THE
SKIPPER

THE
SKIPPER

A Fisherman's Tale

ROGER NOWELL & JEREMY MILLS

Photographs by
DAVID SECOMBE

BCA

LONDON   NEW YORK   SYDNEY   TORONTO

ACKNOWLEDGEMENTS

The television series would not have been possible without the dedication of cameraman Alex Hansen, for whom each trip to sea was a living nightmare, and the rest of the filming team who sensibly stayed on shore, including Lareine Bathe, Martyn Clift, and James Moss. Thanks are due to Paul Hamann for his continued support, and Stefan Ronowicz and Jacky Pointer who worked wonders in the cutting room. At BBC Books Sheila Ableman was brave to commission us, while Martha Caute, Linda Mallory and Linda Blakemore smoothed the process.

Neither project would have been possible without the patience and good humour of the crew of the *William Sampson Stevenson,* on which I spent many happy hours, and her owners W. Stevenson & Sons; or my wife Angela who hopes now to regain me from the sea.

Jeremy Mills

PICTURE CREDITS

All the photographs were taken by David Secombe apart from the following: pages 6, 14, 33, 42, 56, 64, 93, 94, 106, 140, 178 and 182–3 Jeremy Mills; page 169 courtesy Mr and Mrs P. Garnier; page 179 Alex Hansen.

CN 1065

This edition published 1993 by BCA by arrangement with BBC Books, a division of BBC Enterprises Limited

Set in 11 on 13 pt Old Style by Ace Filmsetting Ltd, Frome
Printed and bound in Great Britain by BPCC Paulton Books Ltd
Colour separations by Technik Ltd, Berkhamsted
Jacket printed by Lawrence Allen Ltd, Weston-super-Mare

PREFACE

Walking along Newlyn Quay on my way to the boat one morning, a man came over and started asking about my life at sea. I should know not to talk to strangers because he turned out to be a BBC producer, Jeremy Mills, looking for a trawler skipper to help him make some films about a fishing community. Before I knew what had happened, I'd been well and truly conned into taking part.

Within weeks Jeremy and his cameraman, Alex Hansen, were out with us facing a force nine gale. During the following twelve months they lived on board during several voyages to record our lives at sea. This proved to be a feat of endurance for Alex who spent the first few days of each trip looking white, then green, before he disappeared to the stern of the boat – the old *William Sampson* is not kind to people who suffer from seasickness. I'm sure he wasn't helped by the offers of a good fry up, or the arrival in front of him of the black body bag from the medicine chest, 'Just in case you don't make it,' as our engineer Graham helpfully pointed out.

When the photographer David Secombe joined us the same fate befell him. With both his cameramen indisposed, Jeremy sat up in the wheelhouse with me recording stories and thoughts from my lifetime at sea. We've put them, together with some of the entries and sketches from my log, in this book of tales. It's not a comprehensive guide to fishing, more of a random trawl through my memories triggered by some of the incidents which have happened during this last year. I hope the stories will give you an impression of life for the skipper, the rest of the crew and all our families ashore at a time of great upheaval in the fishing industry.

If nothing else you may look at your fish and chips in a different light.

Roger Nowell, Newlyn 1992

 WELCOME ABOARD THE *William Sampson Stevenson*, **PZ191**, a little old tiger. This is our home for ten days at a time, week in, year out. Our wives would say that with just a couple of days ashore in between trips it's more of a home than our houses. She's 93 feet long and we trawl the seabed in her anywhere from off the Irish coast to down beyond the Isles of Scilly or even up into the North Sea. She's brought us through many a storm of wind, and taken us back into Newlyn with a few good catches in her time.

Let me introduce you to her crew, all local boys from Newlyn and Mousehole who've sailed together for more years than I care to remember; a happy band of men – until we fall out.

Peter 'Mitch' Mitchell is the mate. He's responsible for the running of the deck and keeping all the equipment in working order, as well as storing the fish in the ice hold. We were at primary school together and although he's been on a diet for as long as I've known him, the battle is just about lost now. Mitch was in the merchant navy and tales of trips up exotic rivers are often to be heard when we're out here in a force nine gale. Mitch is well known in the port for the strength of his voice. Great when you're in a

ABOVE Mitch
LEFT The *William Sampson Stevenson* leaving harbour

7

howling gale and you need to be heard the full length of the ship; not so good if he decides to let loose when you're sitting next to him in the galley.

Then there's Graham Inman, our engineer. He has a lot of power on board the ship and we often have to wait for him to say when we can haul in the nets. This has nothing to do with him nurturing the finely tuned engine, but because he's a great football fan. If there's a match on television, especially Leeds United, we have to wait until the game's finished before we can bring in the nets. I know exactly how to needle him. I take the boat out to sea to the point where the television signal becomes weak and wait until the match is well under way. Then just by sailing that little bit further out you can make the signal come and go in a satisfyingly annoying way. Guaranteed to get him going!

Mind you, the oldest member of the crew is just as fussy about when we haul. Bobby Button is sixty-three and I've been fishing with him for nearly thirty years. If hauling is due around meal time I have to make sure he's finished eating well before I call the lads on deck. He won't move until he feels he's had enough time to digest the food. His wife Inez and I have had more than one set-to over the years when we're at sea in poor weather. If we're out in a gale of wind and the phone goes, most times it will be her on the other end, and I know I'm in for an earful. 'What are you doing keeping my poor Bobby out there in weather like this. You should treat them better!' She's often right.

Then there's Geoffrey 'Jiggy' Gilbert. A couple of years back he started behaving very strangely, like a completely different person, niggly all the time. After a while we persuaded him to go to his doctor who did some tests and discovered that he has diabetes. Since he's been receiving treatment he's a changed man, back to his former self and full of fun again. The only thing now is that we have to make sure we don't eat any of his special diabetic jam or jelly, or there's hell on out here.

Then there's Tony Downing, the chef. All I'll say about Tony's cooking is that his wife won't let him cook at home. He has been known to turn up after a couple of days on shore with a bit of a sore head, and we have a special tube of ointment kept ready to cure him of the bed sores which we're convinced he'll get one day. He spends more time in his bunk than his mattress does.

Then there's me, the skipper, Roger Nowell. But that's another story!

ABOVE Graham and Mitch   ABOVE LEFT The skipper in the wheelhouse
OVERLEAF Newlyn Harbour

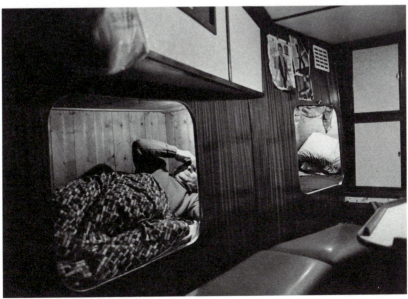

TOP Tony and Jiggy   ABOVE Bobby below in his bunk
LEFT Tony in the galley

ANOTHER 30-FOOT WAVE broke over the *William Sampson*'s bow, sending tons of water cascading along the deck. The three of us in the wheelhouse braced ourselves for the shudder as she lifted her stern out of the water and sent the propeller searching frantically for something to bite on.

This was our fifth day battling against force nine gales which were making fishing impossible and conditions frustrating. When it takes the combined skills of a contortionist, acrobat and British Rail waiter just to pour boiling water from a kettle to make a mug of tea, Newlyn harbour seems a long way off and has a huge appeal.

Fishing has always been a precarious job. It's now supposed to be even more dangerous than mining, and when you're out in these conditions you can see why.

The boys were all pretty fed up. Graham was aft in the galley wedged into the corner trying to watch his wretched football – the picture so snowy he could hardly see a thing. Jiggy went about muttering under his breath and swearing at the beast of the ship. Tony had emerged from his bunk and sat smoking a cigar, preparing himself for cooking yet another meal with pots and pans flying around the galley as though possessed by poltergeists. In the wheelhouse Mitch stood alongside me, his large frame swaying with the motion of the boat. Bobby sat in the skipper's seat watching the waves break, thinking of home and his beloved Inez as he recited the start of the old sailor's poem, 'Every turn of the screw brings me closer to you, my dear,' then nudged me to drive home the point.

I have to agree with him. When the sea's like this and all you're catching is a few lousy soles and a couple of beat-up cod it all seems pointless: 93 feet of steel pounding through the water for no purpose, just to say we're out at sea. You get used to the weather, but not the waste of energy for boat and crew when there's no reason to be here apart from keeping the owner happy. But no skipper likes to be the first to go in for fear that others will stay out making money while they're tied up in port.

We'll be all right, though; the little old tiger's always looked after us well so far, although she's given us a few nail-biting

---

Sorting the catch

moments. The old girl is heavy in her bows because the powerful winch which pulls in the nets is up forward, so sometimes she dives into a big wave and you just wonder whether she's ever going to come up again. You can't show you're worried, though, because the skipper sets the mood for the rest of the crew. If they saw me getting twitchy, they'd start unlashing the liferafts. To be truthful there have been a few times when I've thought my time was up, but deep down I usually think I'll make it. As long as I don't push her into the weather too much she's happy.

These trawlers roll around more than any other type of boat, so in bad weather we leave the trawls down fishing on the seabed as long as possible, like having two moving anchors. If the weather gets too bad to fish we lift the gear until it's just below the surface, acting like stabilizers, and tow along into the weather, waiting for it to pick up. Respect for the sea and the wind is important and you mustn't get too cocky.

The worst thing in poor weather is when you get a trawl stuck on a wreck that you haven't got marked on the charts. (A 'wreck' can be anything from a complete sunken ship to nothing more than a rogue anchor down on the seabed, waiting to trap an unwary skipper.) You have to react quickly. You pull on the warps, steel wires which are attached to the trawls, until they're vertical. Most times that will be enough to help the several tons of trawl unhitch itself as you come above it. But when it doesn't work, you have to just move forward and backward gently, until it lifts itself free. The temptation is to pull away with all the ship's power, but at best this will break something, at worst it can pull you over. Sometimes you can be there for ten, twelve hours just jogging backwards and forwards. The trawl gear's worth at least £10,000, so you have to be careful and patient. The last thing you want is to lose everything by breaking the warp, because then you have to spend the next few hours with a grappling hook on a long line trying to find it all again.

The tide will often do the work for you as it turns and lifts the boat away from the wreck. The main skill required is the ability to imagine what's happening several hundred feet under you. When that trawl comes out of the water after you've raised it successfully, it's exhilarating.

On the other hand, when you've tried your best for hours to get it free but eventually you've lost it, you're the loneliest man in the world up here. You know you've got to face going into the harbour with only one set of gear, and that the crew have got to make up a whole new trawl when they get in. Although they're as good as gold on board here and don't curse me too much, at least not to my face, you know that they've got a lot of work to do. You also know that when you get into harbour the word will soon get around that you've cocked up and it's no consolation to know it wasn't your fault.

We were out off Trevose Head a couple of years back and we looked across and saw a trawler which was heeled over almost on its side. They'd got a trawl stuck on a wreck and as we watched we couldn't believe how clumsily they tried to free themselves. The boat was called *Till Eulenspiegel* from Zeebrugge. She eventually broke the warp and had to go into Newlyn to pick up a new set of gear. The five youngsters on her went straight out again into the Irish Sea. Days later we heard that she'd rolled over and sunk with all hands. The weather was very calm, only about a force three, so she could only either have been run down by another ship, or pulled herself over.

A Belgian minesweeper sent divers down to her, and found her lying on the bottom sitting upright with the gear out intact. It must have been very eerie. There was no sign of damage to the hull, so she couldn't have been run down. One of the nets was full up with what we call creepy crawlies, like starfish, and the only explanation could be that one net became heavy and perhaps stuck in the mud because of these creatures. Then the crew heaved and heaved until they just pulled the boat over. It would only have taken seconds for the deck winch to have been under water, making it difficult for the crew to release the trawls, and then, inevitably, she would have rolled over.

Sad to say that the sinking didn't really surprise us after we'd seen the way they'd handled her before.

Every time you hear about another boat going down it always reminds you of your own mortality. Last time a boat was lost we'd just gone to sea when we heard the news on the radio. The skipper, David something or other, had been trapped in the wheelhouse, while the rest of the crew escaped. The weather conditions were fine and we put it down to another lot of youngsters who'd got a net stuck on a wreck, been stupid and pushed things too hard. But about an hour out of the harbour our phone went and it was my nephew Stephen calling from his trawler to ask if we'd heard about the loss. We talked about it for a while until I asked him if he knew who the boys were. He sounded surprised and said that I knew Tex as well as anyone. The news bulletin had given the skipper's real name, while through all the years we'd sailed and drunk together

17

I'd only ever known him as Tex. He had a vast amount of experience and knew exactly what he was doing, so we couldn't think how it had happened in such calm weather. It really made me wonder what the hell I'm doing out here. If it could happen to a fisherman as skilled as Tex, then it could happen to me.

I'm not really a worrier, but I do care about my wife Nell and daughter Sophie, and wonder what would happen to them if I were to go. I get a bit sorrowful when I lie in my bunk thinking about Sophie at home wondering when her old Dad's coming home and how she would feel if I didn't come back one day. But even that's not enough to make me want to give it up. I go on about how bad the whole fishing business has become, but I still get a great kick out of standing in this wheelhouse on my own of a night and looking around knowing that I am master of all I survey, and have control over my immediate destiny. I enjoy the element of the hunt, wondering if the fish are going to be on the same patch as they were last year, or if they are going to sneak past us.

Despite all our moans we don't have it too bad. Fishermen have never starved, and we certainly don't have it as bad as many others in the world. Bobby and I sometimes sit up here in the wheelhouse yarning about the old times and the old boys and he'll say, 'There's many up Paul Churchyard who'd rather be here.' And as I look out and see the distant lights of other boats I imagine them in their wheelhouses thinking similar thoughts.

One of the hazards which seems to be increasing in frequency is being run down by another boat. Most feared are the huge tankers which take so long to manoeuvre, and often have badly restricted vision. They're usually travelling very fast and can creep up on you unexpectedly, especially if they're coming from behind. According to the rules of the sea in those circumstances they're overtaking and are supposed to give way to fishing boats which are restricted by the nets they're towing. This is all very well in theory, but in practice it's not quite so easy for these large vessels to do anything, even assuming they see you.

I'm afraid some fishing skippers today cut across the bows of great tankers, almost daring them to run them down, but expect to get away with it in a recklessly arrogant way. They might as well lift two fingers. The rule book does say fishing has priority, but it also says that you have to do everything reasonable to avoid collisions – which is often easier said than done.

We were out fishing off the Bishop Rock lighthouse in the Scillies one morning last November when Tony came up to take over the watch. It was about 5.45 A.M. and pitch dark. The radar showed a large vessel coming up behind us and the electronic range scale gave it a distance of about three miles.

I'd been watching the ship's bearing which hadn't changed although it was getting a lot closer, a sure sign of a collision course. So I eased the power back to slow us down, hoping that would give the ship room to pass ahead of us. I couldn't do much more because our nets were being towed along the bottom.

Within moments the ship was just a mile away. I shouted a warning down to the galley and by the time Jiggy had gone to the aft door to look out, it was upon us. It was so close that if I'd stood on the end of the derrick I could have touched it. Even in the dark as it steamed past us at what we worked out was about seventeen knots I could look up and read the name on her stern, *Gina, Limassol*.

As soon as it passed I got on the VHF radio. 'Didn't you see me?' After a short delay a voice came back, 'I didn't know what you were. I call, call, call!'

Well we never heard him, and in any case he was the overtaking vessel so he should have given way. I was furious and told him I'd report the incident. He never came back on the radio. When I reported it to the coastguard they said there wasn't much they could do, but they'd forward it to the Department of Trade and Industry who would then make out a report.

They then wanted me to supply them with a chart and all the details, but I just felt it was all pretty hopeless and a waste of time. The report on the investigation into the loss of the Newlyn boat *Margaret and William II* the previous September had just been published, and it seemed to me they'd been in much the same situation as us except that tragically they had been hit, were sunk and had lost two of the crew. I'll never forget the mate Ian Hague telling the story of what had happened.

The boat was a little wooden drift netter about thirty-three feet long. They'd been down south-west of the Wolf Rock off the Isles of Scilly picking up the last of her nets before returning to Newlyn. It was about five o'clock in the evening and they were steaming along at about four or five knots. Ian and the skipper, Malcolm, were sitting in the wheelhouse, while Dennis (Malcolm's brother) and Alex, the two members of the crew, were below sleeping, as was Terry, a young lad who'd gone out for a trial trip with them to see how he got on at sea.

Suddenly Ian registered a look of horror on Malcolm's face.

19

Looking up, Ian saw an orange wall towering over the wheelhouse and he shouted, 'Boat!' As he shouted there was an almighty crash. The next second everything was dark and he was under the water. He was sure he was doing to die, but something in him seemed to say 'Fight!'

He kicked his legs and thrashed his arms, which took him to the surface. When he emerged he saw a large cargo boat with an orange hull steaming away from them, and he was surrounded by bits and pieces of fishing gear floating in the water. Malcolm had already come to the surface and he shouted, 'The liferaft's behind you!' Ian says he doesn't know why, but he shouted back, 'Young Terry Freeman's gone.' But then Terry floated to the surface. Ian swam over to the liferaft and pulled the cord to inflate it, hoping all the time that the other two would come up as well.

Ian was wearing all his fishing gear and found it hard to get into the liferaft; the young lad had been resting below and only had jeans and a T-shirt on. Malcolm swam towards the bows of the *Margaret and William II* which by then were pointing vertically with the other two-thirds of the boat under the water. As Ian and Terry struggled into the liferaft they realized they were drifting away from Malcolm, so they leaned out and paddled furiously with their hands. By the time they reached him Malcolm was struggling – he'd been in the water for quite a while. All the time they kept hoping that the other two would suddenly float to the surface.

Seeing the orange hull of the cargo ship getting smaller very quickly, Ian grabbed a rocket flare but because of the panic he fired it into the sea. The visibility was quite good, about a mile and a half, so they could still just see the cargo ship. A second flare went off up into the sky and they waited, expecting the ship to respond at any second. But there was no reaction and they could only watch as it sailed out of sight.

Ian wrapped himself in bandages to keep warm and they drifted through the night. It must have been pretty terrifying with the waves slapping against the bottom of the liferaft.

The next morning they saw what looked like a tanker about three-quarters of a mile away. Ian grabbed a couple of hand flares and set them off. The tanker made a signal of three blasts on the horn, so they assumed they'd been seen. It looked as though it was slowing down, but then it seemed to pick up again before disappearing from view. They knew that it takes a long time for these vessels to stop, so they kept on hoping. As time went on they didn't see or hear anything more of it.

They had plenty of water, and were talking about how long they might be in the liferaft, when they heard an aircraft. There was no way of telling whether it was searching, or just a passenger plane flying over. Within minutes it came back and as it flew low over them they saw it was a Nimrod. It must have been the most welcome sight imaginable. In the end they were picked up by a navy helicopter from Culdrose after being in the sea for twenty-two hours.

The results of the Department of Transport investigation didn't go down too well in Newlyn.

The captain of the Dutch chemical tanker *Jacobus Broere* contacted the coastguard when he heard that a boat had gone down at a position and time which corresponded with his route. The investigators found paint scraped along the side of the tanker of the same colour as the hull of the *Margaret and William*. There wasn't any doubt that the two had been in collision, but the report seemed to put the cause of the accident on both ships in equal proportion, saying that they should both have been keeping a better watch and have seen each other. It made most of us think that it really wasn't worth getting involved in reporting near misses in the future when they didn't seem to be able to do anything even after two lives had been lost.

Mind you, there are some boats around which don't help our cause. They've had their sterns filled to give them weather cover in such a design that there's no way they could ever see aft, and they wouldn't see anything approaching from behind until it was too late. Keeping watch on some of them must be a bit like driving a car without any wing mirrors and with the back seat piled so high that you can't see out of the window. On a calm day it's bad enough, but in conditions like tonight's storm it's a real lash-up on some of those boats.

As the *William Sampson* dived into yet another thundering wave, Bobby muttered to himself fiercely, 'We're worse off than convicts out here.' It's an opinion he's offered several times over the years we've sailed together. On a night like this, with the weather getting worse by the hour, I think he's probably right. It's time to turn round and look for some shelter.

OVERLEAF Newlyn harbour, low tide

 AN ALMIGHTY BANG brought Graham running up the ladder from the deck. We'd just started to bring in the nets when the winch engine, which operates all the various bits of rope and wire to shoot and haul, had decided it wanted to become the centre of attention by blowing up. Graham was furious, almost as though he was dealing with a naughty child who'd deliberately got itself into trouble. He shut everything down and stormed below to the engine room to survey the damage. Things were not good: it looked as though one of the pistons had disintegrated, with no hope of any repairs out at sea. We sat there in the water, unable to lift the nets and wondering whether we would have to call for assistance, until Graham worked out a way of transferring power from the main engine to the winch. We then had enough power to raise the nets. Instead of the usual fifteen minutes to pull the gear up from the seabed, it would take us several hours, but at least it was better than having to call on another boat to come alongside for us to use its winch, a complicated operation at the best of times, let alone in the dark.

With the nets aboard we set course for Newlyn where the shore gang could take the engine apart to assess the damage. Graham was unusually subdued; I could tell he felt responsible, almost embarrassed, even though there was nothing he could have done to stop it happening. Jiggy and Bobby were trying not to look too pleased at the prospect of an extra day or two in port.

The trouble is that the engine's so old they don't make spares for it any more and I knew that whatever we ended up doing would be a lash-up requiring some time in port.

At first light we landed the few boxes of fish we'd caught in our brief time out. The shore gang came aboard leaving us nothing to do but wait, so we went up to the Ship Inn for a pint.

All was not bad news. Even though we'd come in after only four days out, it was a Tuesday and not many others were selling on the market so prices were up; even more for our fish which was fresh. We made the same as we might expect with more boxes from a saturated market. If we can get out again before too long we might even do quite well out of this misfortune: an extra day in port and more money for our catch.

We were sharing out the money in the pub, having a few beers, when Tony the Spaniard came in with a bag of salt fish. We usually try to give Tony some small pollack every so often. He soaks it in the sort of rough salt we used to use for salting down nets, leaves it in a bucket for two or three days then dries it in the sun. When it's dried he cuts it up in pieces and brings it into the pub, where it goes perfectly with a pint, like the fishy equivalent of pork scratchings. Salt cod's another of Tony's favourites, especially the tail end where it's thinner and there are never any worms. It gets nice and dry and is easy to break up. Very small megrims are good for salting as well. You see the Spanish boats out at sea preparing them by taking the head and tail off before tying them up around the stern to dry. If Tony's enthusiasm is anything to go by you can see why the Spanish boats risk all the fines for catching and hiding away undersize fish, because it's considered such a delicacy back home in Spain.

There are several other parts of the catch which usually find their way into the pub. I'm always happy to catch cuttlefish, for example, because there's a lady down the road from me in Goldsithney who cooks them in their own ink, then brings them across the road to the Crown, and they are flippin' delicious. Before you know it a group has gathered around and you end up not getting any to eat yourself.

Jiggy and Tony in the Star

Squid is another favourite. Take the backbone out and you're left with a sort of torpedo tube which can be stuffed with scallops, the open end tied up, then fried. You slice it up and serve rings of squid surrounding slices of scallops. You've got to have fresh squid, mind you, otherwise it can be like eating rubber bands.

Tony often talks about the way they catch octopus in the Mediterranean, and I've always fancied trying my hand at it. They have little thistle-shaped jars which they string out in long lines. The octopus backs its body into the jar and they just pull out the pots with the creatures inside. The female octopus crawls in there to have her young and then dies so they can catch them pretty easily that way.

We had a good old session in the pub, what with the landing money, the beer and Tony's salt fish. I could listen to him for hours, in fact if I remember correctly I think I did. Tony arrived in Newlyn having escaped from Spain by boat after his assassination attempt on Franco failed, and he's been here ever since. I fished with him on several boats, and in his time he was one of the best hands you could hope to sail with. His skills at mending nets were legendary.

He was a bit quick with his knife in other ways as well. He was on watch once with all hands turned in when we came fast on a wreck. On this particular boat you had to rush out on deck and release the winch to stop the boat being pulled under. When the skipper, George Lacey, came running out of the cabin to take charge, the first thing he saw on the wheelhouse chair was a copy of *Parade*, a fairly tame girlie magazine. He immediately assumed that the reason we'd come fast was that Tony hadn't been concentrating on the watch, but had been too interested in looking at other things. After we'd cleared the gear off the wreck Tony, who was still crouched on the deck operating the winch, felt something falling on his head like confetti. When he realized that it was his magazine torn up into tiny pieces he went mad, cursing and swearing at George. He swung round and made for the wheelhouse, grabbing his knife which was so sharp you could shave with it. 'I'll kill the bastard!' he was yelling – and he would have. I leapt across the deck, shouting after him to stop. Tony was a big strong man, and if I hadn't broken the spell he would have been up there at George, and I wouldn't have liked to witness what would have been left of our poor skipper. Then as quickly as he'd got mad he calmed down, and within the hour they were friends again.

It must be the Latin blood, because I've had similar fun sailing with another immigrant to Newlyn. In the summertime we used to sit out on the stern of the boat eating crab, which was always a favourite food, everyone liking them cooked slightly differently. Portuguese Joe liked eating his with alternate mouthfuls of raw sweet onion from his personal supply which he kept in his locker.

We were out there one day eating our crabs, sitting around the punt which was laughingly meant to be our liferaft, but was full of coal and bags of spuds. We wore thigh length seaboots which you'd turn down when you weren't working, leaving a sort of bag around your knee, and when Portuguese Joe went below to get his onion I hid his crab claw in the fold of my boot, thinking it would be a bit of a laugh.

When he came back to find his delicacy gone he said to me, 'Hey, boy, where's my crab claw?' I said that I didn't know where it was so he turned to lay into another young deckie, John. Before long they were calling each other all the names under the sun, holding each other so their faces were just inches apart, the spit flying like venom. Then Portuguese Joe grabbed his fish gutting knife, held it behind John's ear, and said that he'd cut it off if John didn't tell him where his food had gone.

While the other crew member, Ernie, was killing himself laughing, I was shaking with fear because I'd started all this. They were really laying into each other, so I tipped the crab out of my boot and shouted, 'Hang on, Joe, here it is,' pointing to the deck.

Released from the threat of Joe's knife, John turned on me shouting, 'You bastard, you did that!' and took a swing. But I was quicker, ducked and laid one on him, sending him smack against the stern of the boat, then scat him over the punt into the coal.

He went up to the wheelhouse crying up to the skipper, Whackers, who was six foot six and a big powerful man. Without saying anything Whackers strode aft, grabbed my jacket, lifted me clean off the deck, and flung me down on the coal. Then he pulled out his knife and put it against my neck. 'I'll cut your bloody throat if you start something like that again!' Out of the corner of my eye I could see Ernie killing himself. We were only young boys really, and I couldn't quite believe that my life could come so near to ending over a crab claw.

Crabs ready for market

28

Food tends to take an extra importance out at sea, because it's one of the few breaks in the day's monotony. Ernie and Portuguese Joe used to save all the whelks from the net until they had a big beef kettle full of them, which they would boil up. They'd take their cooked whelks forward under the whaleback and eat them like you would a packet of crisps as they were working. These whelks weren't cleaned and prepared like the ones you buy on the seafront: Ernie and Joe would eat everything, including the sand bag and the gut. Another chap used to have cooked crab claws strung round his neck on a piece of string, and every so often while he was on watch he'd crack one of these on the wheel and nibble away at it.

There's nothing worse for morale than a bad meal. We had a cook on one boat called Charlie Brown, whose first meal at sea every trip was always disgusting. We didn't have a table in the galley, but had to eat down below in the cabin. As soon as we started to steam off to the fishing grounds we would turn in, only to be woken an hour or so later by the sound of the large beef kettle being brought down the ladder and being placed on the table with a loud clatter. Charlie would put the plates out around the table

In the galley of the *William Sampson*

30

with great ceremony and shout, 'Come and get it, you lovely boys!' in his gruff Lowestoft accent. Every trip we lived in hope that it would be different. Every trip we were disappointed. We'd sit waiting for the skipper to come below, then Charlie would open the lid with a flourish, the skipper would take one look, groan and go straight back up to his cabin and we'd climb back into our bunks without even needing to look. Sausage soup again. This speciality was made with a tin of tomatoes, a raw onion and ordinary uncooked sausages, all put in the saucepan together and boiled for a few minutes. It was consistently inedible.

At sea we would sit down to his Lowestoft version of Cornish pasties. He was well known throughout Newlyn for these, which were just as disgusting as his sausage soup. They were thin like a pancake, had no turnip, but masses of pepper. For hours afterwards you were good for nothing, while your guts rumbled and complained away.

Charlie was a huge man, over six foot six but thin as a rake. He couldn't have weighed more than seven stone. Thinking back to his food I suppose that wasn't surprising. When it was his duty to look over the rail, shouting as the nets surfaced, he was so tall that he could kneel and still see over the top.

He was a terrible joker. You'd go down after shooting the nets, take off your clothes and jump into your bunk only to jump out again when your back landed on a tin of ham or a jar of coffee. Then he would create hell, swearing blind that someone had nicked all his supplies.

He always used to take his teeth out to clean them at night and one time he lost them. Years later we were out on the stern lifting up some old chain and there underneath was a broken mug with his teeth grinning back at us. Mind you, I sailed with one old boy who would come down the pier in his shiny suit, climb aboard, take his teeth out and put them into the pocket of his suit where they would stay until we went ashore. This meant that for the whole trip no one could understand a word he said. Without his teeth his mouth was so rubbery that he could pull his lower lip right up over his nose.

There was a cook I sailed with on another boat who made Charlie look like a three star chef. In the old days before we wore gloves on deck the oilskins used to chafe the skin terribly around your wrists. This chafed area would be irritated by the water and sand, making the skin go red, then form huge sea-boils which filled with pus before dropping off. There was nothing you could do to

31

avoid them; the only treatment was to wear a flannel bandage. For some reason white flannel didn't work; it was only the red type, which the store sold in three-foot lengths. You'd wrap a bandage around each wrist and hold it together with a piece of tape. When you came off the deck you'd take your bandages off, run them in clean water and hang them up to dry.

When this particular cook, Jumbo Smith King, came off the deck he would give his bandages a cursory rinse before hanging them over the cooker. He always made a stew which would bubble away on top of the stove for hours. This one evening we were all sat around waiting for the skipper to come down to get his before we were served. The old man went across to the stove, put a ladleful of stew on his plate, looked at it then screamed, 'What the hell is this!' One of Charlie's red flannels had fallen into the pot. The skipper flung the bandage and the stew out the door and stomped off back to the wheelhouse.

Jumbo was such a dirty old boy. He would kneel in the pound gutting fish, which meant he'd end up with slime and guts covering his legs and all around him, smoking his pipe all the while. One day I watched with disbelief as the pipe fell out of his mouth right down into this mess and he simply picked it up, gave it a shake and put it straight back in his mouth.

I have an obsession about cleanliness on board ship. Just because we live in these conditions doesn't mean we have to behave like pigs, and, even sitting in the pub, thinking about that cook again made me feel queasy. I had another pint to take away the taste.

We were settling in for a real session when Graham came in looking pleased. They'd managed to find a spare piston from a redundant engine and we could go back to sea tomorrow. Jiggy and Bobby were dejected. 'What a lash-up!' was the only comment they could muster.

———————

I'D JUST WORKED out the answer to one across in the *Fishing News* crossword when I was disturbed by a shout on the radio. '*William Sampson*, this is *Celtic Mor*. Are you reading me?' I took my feet off the rail and picked up the VHF handset to reply. The *Celtic Mor* is a small crabber which works round the south coast. Although I've never met the skipper, Robert, we've often spoken on the radio in the middle of the night, spending hours chatting away about anything and everything as we do out here. As he spoke I looked on the radar and saw the small blip, indicating his boat fast approaching us. In a dejected voice he warned that we were just about to run into a line of his crab pots, giving me the lat and long readings of where they lay. Muttering all sorts of obscenities, I immediately turned the boat hard around, away from the positions he'd given, in order to run along parallel with them. I thought I'd avoided them, but when I rushed to the window I could just see the buoy which marked the end of one of his lines being dragged along by our port warp.

The language on the radio would have breached most international codes, but I told him that we would haul the nets to see what else we'd caught. The crabbers string out several miles of pots and

if we'd caught the middle of that lot we could be towing it all behind us and he stood to lose thousands of pounds' worth of gear.

There was a deep swell with a fair bit of wind and as he came alongside us he disappeared from view with every rolling wave. His bows leapt in the air, then crashed down again, making a spectacular sight in amongst the white horses of the breaking crests. I called the boys to come on deck to haul.

I'd been watching another larger radar echo moving steadily towards us, on a course to pass very close. It had been at a safe distance from us while we'd been towing along quietly. Within moments, however, we'd completely changed our direction and were on a heading which would take us across the tanker's bow. If I wanted to avoid the crab pots I would have to continue this course until we came to the end of the line when I could turn back away from the tanker. With every passing minute the tanker bore down on us steadily, and suddenly the vast expanses of the ocean became as small as a swimming pool.

I looked again at the position of Robert's gear, then at the course of the tanker, and realized I could just about take avoiding action as soon as we cleared the end of his line. Then I noticed that if I did turn to starboard I would tow right into a wreck. Turning to port would present an even larger target for the tanker to hit, so I had no choice but to keep on course, ease back our speed, and say a quick prayer. The tanker was now only a few hundred yards away from us. I could read her name without binoculars and see the huge wave formed as her bulbous bow thrust the water aside.

She passed ahead of us at a frightening speed, towering over us. The *Celtic Mor* had steamed to the other end of his pots to check them, and as the tanker drew away the little crabber looked like a small colourful cork bobbing up and down beside it.

As soon as this minor crisis was over we started to haul the gear, fearful of what we might find. Graham stomped about on the deck, his face thunderous with fury at the waste of time and effort. 'These crabbers shouldn't expect anything else if they shoot on trawling ground!' he shouted as he threw the hammer on to the deck. With the beams alongside we could see that the line attached to the buoy was well and truly wound around our gear, but Robert came on the radio saying that they'd found the other end so we must have just cut the line, and his pots were intact. After a lot of cursing and swearing Graham managed to flick the buoy off our gear and throw it out away from the boat, leaving the men on the *Celtic Mor* to wind it in. It was a lucky escape all round.

 WE'VE JUST RETURNED from fishing up in the North Sea, chasing the fish as they move around the waters. It's just about the only way I can tell the seasons are passing out here, apart from slightly worse conditions in the winter.

The boys were none too happy by the end of our time up north. It's all right for me up here in the wheelhouse but working on deck the cold weather certainly makes life pretty miserable for them. Jiggy kept shaking his craggy head at me, 'Too far away from Mummy, Roger!' I had to agree: it felt as though I hadn't seen Sophie and Nell for weeks.

The fishing's more difficult as well, with a very different type of seabed to deal with than in our own home waters. You tow up great sheets of Moor Log, a peaty substance which is the stage before coal. It fills the nets and jams everything up so you have to cut it up with a shovel. Fish gravitate towards it because it's full of worms, but it's a heck of a job to clear the decks when you land a big chunk of it. You pick up all sorts of weed in the North Sea as well. Some of it affects your skin, making you come out in a rash, or itch like mad. All of it's a real pain to clear from the nets.

Tempers were getting very short. Several times I leant out of the wheelhouse window and caught Graham, his face taut with anger, swearing away at Tony for not being quick enough with the net release. As always Tony remained impassive, even slightly bewildered, letting it all wash over him, while Jiggy looked on from the other side of the deck screeching with laughter. They work in pairs on both nets, one operating the ropes while the other empties the cod end of fish. Bobby and Jiggy have worked together on the starboard side for so many years they're like an old married couple, finding fault with everything the other does. It was Graham's turn to look across and roar with laughter as Jiggy muttered and swore at Bobby. I don't know how they'd pass the time if they couldn't shout at each other.

We were all glad to get home for a couple of days to see our families and now to be back here down off the Cornish coast again. You don't get any Moor Log here, but the nets end up full of rocks or snagged on wrecks instead. The debris on the seabed must show the history of seagoing craft, from the sailing ships which foundered on the treacherous reefs, through the remains of

convoys which fell foul of the German U-boats based in Brest during the war, to more recent victims.

In 1975 when the Russian fleet was fishing around here a new wreck was added. One of their factory ships went aground up on the Seven Stones reef near the Isles of Scilly, chasing what they thought was a shoal of fish, but which turned out to be the rocks. They discovered their mistake too late. I went up alongside in our ship to have a good look at her hard fast on the rocks. The crew weren't in any great danger: in fact they even had all the lifeboats out transferring everything valuable to another Russian ship. It was amazing to see the large number of women on board, employed to gut fish.

We've books full of the positions of these wrecks or even an odd bit of gear that another boat's lost. All of them are capable of ruining the nets, but most of them also hide fish so it's always tempting to get as close as you dare.

All hands take their turn on the four-hour watches between hauls, supposedly steering the boat along a track I've laid on the plotter, but each has their own favourite style which reflects their personality. Graham is the mischievous maverick: he likes to push things as far as possible, dodging right in around wrecks, risking damage to the nets in the hope of those few extra fish. I know he does it even though he tries to get back on my course before waking me up to haul. Mitch is the opposite, he's a stickler for obeying my last order to the letter in true seaman's style. Jiggy can be a bit devilish, and likes to make diversions to revisit pieces of ground where he's found fish in the past. He divides his attention between these sorties and talking to his sons-in-law on the radio. He's always worried that they're getting more fish than we are and if he thinks they're doing well he tries to persuade me to go and join them. Bobby just likes to sit listening to Radio Cornwall and doesn't worry too much about anything, but just steams along quietly. Tony goes up and down oblivious to everything apart from that line on the chart and the endless cigars he smokes.

There was all hell let loose on the deck this morning after Jiggy's watch because the nets came in full of shells and hardly any fish. As I saw the nets come over the side heavy with rubbish I knew there'd be trouble, and Graham didn't let me down. 'Not concentrating on the job in hand, too busy talking on the radio!' he shouted from inside the net where he was pulling out the few fish which had been trapped. Yesterday the net was full of stones after Bobby's watch and it was much the same, 'Too many skippers in the wheelhouse!' digging at the fact that Bobby and I had been up there putting the world to rights for the whole of his watch. There are always more allegations and counter allegations flying across the deck than there are fish.

Down here off the south-west coast we catch virtually every species of fish from cod, haddock and sole, to hake, monkfish and conger eels. Even scallops, crabs and lobsters are brought up from the seabed by the trawls. You're never really surprised at what comes up in the net. One of the skippers had a Ford Escort, another an elephant which had fallen overboard from a cargo ship. We've quite often towed up pelvic bones, which are easy to spot because their shape stands out in the catch. Usually they're old and brown, but you sometimes get them all white and clean, from some poor yachtsman who's been lost not so long before.

We once had a terrible shock when a skin diver was pulled up in the net. The lads called me down to the deck and with trepidation I went across to take a look at the figure. It was lying face down with most of the catch on top of it. The black frogman's outfit was shiny, the flippers still in place, but there was no sign of the air bottles. I thought I'd got it this time, my first body. I'd heard horror stories from other skippers of bodies which had been in the sea for a while, and knew that it could be a pretty unpleasant sight, with the prolonged effects of submersion rotting the flesh. The crew were all looking at me, so there was nothing for it. Gingerly I put my hand underneath to turn the body on to its back. It was rigid. Nothing for it but to flip it over. It was horrible, we all jumped back at the sight of the contorted features grinning back at us through the covering of seaweed. Then I looked again. We'd been prepared for something horrendous, but hadn't been pre-pared for a victim which would have been more at home in a Burton's shop window than a mortuary. My first body was a dummy in full frogman's outfit. We discovered later that it was used by the navy for practising underwater rescue techniques. On our way back into Newlyn we tied him to the bow of our boat like a strange figurehead.

There's more going on above and under the sea than is worth thinking about too closely. Michael Hoskin, a skipper from Penzance, was out on the deck having a pee over the side one day, out in the middle of nowhere, when he looked up to find a periscope staring back at him.

The Newlyn boat *St Clair*, PZ199, was one of the first trawlers to catch a submarine. The engineer, Archie Swan, was on deck throwing some oily rags over the side when he noticed that the boat was being towed sideways and backwards, although the engines were pulling ahead at full power. Moments later this great black shape surfaced alongside, with their nets draped across her like some sort of failed camouflage. At least they got their nets back.

The PZ199 was later sold to someone in the Solomon Islands and the number given to a new boat in Newlyn, the *Algrie*. To everyone's surprise eight years ago this new boat was fishing off the Wolf Rock lighthouse with my nephew Stephen as mate when she caught another sub. Stephen ran up to the wheelhouse and released the trawls before they could be pulled over or towed under. They then had to spend the next day towing a line with a grappling hook on the end to try and recover the gear. The television news sent a cameraman out in a helicopter, and there on the box that evening was a beautiful shot of the *Algrie*, with 'Hello Mum' picked out on her deck in large letters made from rolls of pink loo paper!

We've been out fishing in the past when a British submarine has surfaced near us and shouted across to us for some fish. We've steamed right under the bows of the awesome beast and given them a few mackerel in return for a couple of packets of cigarettes and perhaps the odd bottle. We were quite used to swopping things with the navy – sometimes a helicopter from the Royal Naval Air Station at Culdrose used to hover above us, lower a line, and we'd send up a basket of fish to them in return for the papers.

Most of the interesting items which are brought up from the depths originally came from one or other of the armed forces. It wasn't that long ago that we towed up the undercarriage of what must have been a huge American World War II bomber with a wheel as big as I'm tall. Someone said to me at the time that we should have gone back and towed into the wreck a few more times because they reckoned that during the war the planes flew so high they had to use mercury in the hydraulics, so the units would have been worth something as scrap. I wasn't so sure about that, so we stuck to trawling for fish.

We've towed up great huge stainless steel powervanes used by the navy in mine-sweeping, and even more ominous clutter.

We were out there last year when Mitch came down to me in the galley in quite a panic.

'There's a mine out here!' I told him to bugger off.

'I'm telling you, there's a mine out here!' I went up on deck expecting a practical joke, but sure enough there was a mine floating towards us. It was like something out of an old war movie. I thought to myself, 'This actually is a mine, God help us!'

We tried to keep it in sight but at a reasonable distance while I called up Falmouth coastguard on the radio.

'Now look, don't think I'm taking the mickey or trying to be funny or anything, but we've got a mine alongside us.'

The reply came: 'Wait one,' and I could imagine the bloke on the other end trying to remember the training session which had covered mines at sea.

'What is your position?'

I gave them our latitude and longitude and they asked if we could go alongside and secure it. It occurred to me that they just wanted to know where we were in case things went a bit wrong, a thought which didn't add to my confidence. We didn't know whether this thing was dangerous or not, and I wasn't too eager to prove how brave I was. But they persuaded me that it would probably be safe and that I really should go alongside and get some ropes around it.

I compared it with all the First and Second World War mines we'd towed up when I was young. This thing seemed brand new, painted black with white writing on its casing. There were no signs of any plungers on it, but I knew from ones we'd towed up before that some of them were magnetic.

There was something less intimidating about the ones I'd seen years back. Perhaps it was partly the bravado of youth, but we used to get them on deck and open them. The detonator was in the middle surrounded by packs of explosive with 'BOCM one and a quarter pounds' written on them. They looked like blocks of butter with the texture of papier mâché. There was great excitement when we removed these, tore off a strip, crumbled it on to the top of the stove and watched it crackle and sparkle like powerful indoor fireworks. It cheered up our days at sea.

This modern, efficient-looking brute was a different story. We carefully put a strop around it and lifted it on to the deck. All hands went a bit quiet during this operation. I reckon they thought the skipper had lost his marbles. We carried on working, the lads avoiding the corner of the deck where the mine sat. After quite a delay the coastguard came back over the radio in cheerful mood. He told us they'd spoken to the navy who'd agreed it was one they'd lost. This seemed careless of them.

'Oh, by the way, it's only a dummy used for minesweeping practice!'

There was relief on board then. We kept it on deck so that we could take it back to Newlyn, and fishing continued.

You won't believe this, but what happened next day? We were towing along and there bobbing in the water towards us was another one of these black mines. It joined the first on deck and we took both of them back into harbour, and put them on the pier for the navy to pick up. We never had a word of acknowledgement from them, not a letter or a phone call to thank us for saving what must have been a few quids' worth of gear.

Back in the Sixties we were picking up all sort of bombs left over from the war, especially off Falmouth. Many a time a trawler's been towing along when out of the blue, 'Boom!' the boat's lifted out of the sea because the trawl has hit some sort of explosive.

I can't help wondering if some of the boats which have disappeared mysteriously have been lost after towing up bombs or mines. You're not allowed to throw them back. You're supposed to contact the coastguard and if you're not happy about taking the mine back into port you've to lower it carefully to the seabed, note the position and let the navy come out and make it safe.

You never know what's going to come up in the nets – we get all sorts of things. Ten years ago I was out fourteen miles south of

Checking a net for damage

the Longships lighthouse when we hauled the gear, undid the net, and a small white container about the size of a hardback book fell out. We couldn't see very clearly what was inside because it was full of sand, but on the back was etched, 'Property of the Home Office if found contact . . .' and a number. When we washed the sand away we found it held four test tubes. We cleaned them up a bit more, revealing black etched printing on what looked like white plastic. Three of the labels meant nothing to us, but the fourth read Mustard Gas. Not really the words you want to read on a test tube when you're holding it in your hands and the sea is throwing the boat around. I knew it would be a darn sight more than spilt milk if that lot took off across the deck.

I wrapped the damn thing up in my towel to cushion it, and put it in the locker under my bunk. I was afraid to throw it overboard in case it broke or we towed it up again.

We were out for several more days and after we'd landed the fish I went up to the pub to sort the lads' money out and have a drink. It wasn't until a couple of pints later that I remembered the container which was sitting under the pile of other blokes' bags in the corner of the pub. I couldn't be bothered with all the Home Office numbers so I phoned the local police station in Penzance and told them what I'd found out at sea. There was a silence on the other end. They asked where I was and when I told them I was in the pub there was a bit more of a silence. I said, 'Well, it's been out there rolling around the ship for a few days. It's hardly going to come to any harm here all wrapped up in my bag.'

Before long a police car turned up. I wanted to give the box to them so I could stay and have a bit of a chat with the lads, but no, they weren't going to go off with it on their own. So they made me sit in the back of the panda car and hold it while they drove cautiously up to the police station. While we were going along I had another good look at the test tubes. It was amazing how new they looked. We often dredge up old bottles which have been on the seabed for years getting scratched and chipped by the movement of the sand, but this was different. The tubes looked brand new and inside you could clearly see all the crystals in place. At the police station they all discussed what they should do. I didn't mind too much – I just wanted to get off.

They decided that I had to sign a bit of paper before they put the container in the safe. As far as I was concerned that was that: I went back to the pub and never gave it much more of a thought.

Not long after this I was at home relaxing when away went the phone. It was Dougie Williams, the local reporter, asking me what I'd been up to because a team from HMS *Drake* in Plymouth had arrived in town at great speed to pick up this box thing and they were now all over Newlyn asking questions. They were trying to find out more about where it had been picked up and what we'd been doing at the time.

I went back over to the harbour and had a chat to them. They listened for a while then said, 'Oh, it's from a First World War wreck.'

I couldn't understand this because the thing was in perfect condition, not scratched at all, and I couldn't believe that it had been down there for seventy years.

'Oh yes,' they said, 'you must have towed into a wreck and opened up a store room.' They went on to explain that this white box was made from Bakelite which I'd always thought was brown. It looked more like modern plastic to me, but I'm no expert. I wondered why it hadn't faded over that length of time or even broken up, but they didn't really have an answer and I didn't like to argue.

Then Dougie came back on the phone and asked a bit more about it, and suddenly we all started to wonder whether it might have come from Nancekuke, the well guarded ministry of defence research station on the cliffs above Portreath, around the coast from St Ives. The rumours got printed in the papers, all the speculation was denied by officials and we didn't hear anything more about it. I suppose we'll never know where it came from, but it made me think about what else might be lurking out there on the seabed.

Listening to the news on the radio, Greenpeace are making a fuss about what they say are large quantities of explosives being dumped by the government 400 miles off Land's End. They say that it's all being done now to beat a European ban on the dumping of waste at sea due to come into effect soon, so maybe we're in for a few more interesting catches around here in the future.

AS I WAS WALKING along by the Seamen's Mission on my way to the boat, a man came over and asked if I was Roger Nowell. I was immediately suspicious, expecting him to be from the tax office or something equally horrible. He introduced himself as Robert from the *Celtic Mor* crabber. He thanked me for our help when we'd snagged his pots and then grabbed me by my collar and told me not to do it again. For one awful moment I thought there'd be trouble, but he laughed, and when he explained that he'd just had a whole set of gear towed away by another trawler I could hardly blame him for getting upset. He's been in touch on the radio several times since the incident, giving us his readings so we can avoid the gear. If we all worked together like that there'd be no problems.

Leaving harbour, I noticed three young lads sitting on the end of the pier. When I blew the hooter as we went through the gaps they glanced up, before returning their attention to the seagulls they'd been taunting with stones. At their age I'd have been one of a score of boys watching the boats go to sea; these days it's rare to see any youngsters taking an interest in the comings and goings.

After we'd passed Mousehole Island and Jiggy had finished the ritual of blowing the hooter to his family ashore, the lads went below to turn in while we steamed the eight hours or so to our fishing grounds. Mitch stayed up in the wheelhouse with me talking about how things have changed over the years since he and I were at school together.

School was just an interruption to time spent in the harbour, and doesn't hold many memories for me, although those I do have are happy. The infants' school I attended is now an artist's studio, and the one image I have is of milk being delivered in winter. We'd line up the small bottles along the fenders of the two open fires at either side of the room. The creamy top would get all hot and the bottom would still be cold. Quite disgusting really.

The headmistress, Miss Harvey, always reminded me of old Queen Mary with her hair all piled up on her head in a bun, golden specs and very frail. Years later when we studied for our mates' tickets in Newlyn the teacher was Captain Harvey, her brother.

I only ever missed two days' schooling, and that was because I was out in a boat with my brother Frank when we got caught in a gale of wind up off Trevose, and couldn't get back to harbour.

Almost as soon as we'd learnt to walk, all our spare time was spent on the old quay with the Old Man, mucking about in small boats. When he was away I went out in the local baker's boat, laying and hauling crab pots. By the time we were in our teens we were going out on our own around St Michael's Mount or beyond, working the lines in small twenty-five footers to catch mackerel or a few pollack. While we were out there feathering or spinning we'd see the old trawlers go out. I was never in any doubt that I would end up on one, it was just a case of when. How much pestering would my elder brother Frank put up with before he gave in?

Frank was mate on a trawler and every time he came in to land his fish I would go down to the quay to help. He'd give me a couple of bob to scrub the hold and fish baskets. I'd look at the massive trawls all strung up along the side of the boat and try to imagine what they would look like when they were working.

I'd seen my Old Man using a small trawl, just a few feet long. He used to tell me how fishermen would travel up to Kent or Sussex on the train, with these trawls slung over their shoulders when they went away to fish. As I listened to his stories, a whole magical world began to develop in my head.

I was twelve when my pestering finally worked. Frank agreed to take me out on a long trip. I can remember the feeling of excitement in my stomach at the prospect of leaving the harbour on my first real voyage. Some of my pals were going out with their brothers or dads and we were all full of it, swaggering down the pier, 'Look at us, we're going out with the big men in the big boats.'

I can smell that boat now, leaking diesel, rotting fish, and the old coal fire. It was not the journey I'd hoped it would be. By the time we'd rounded Land's End the swaggering had changed to staggering. Die, did I die? I became oblivious to everything except Brother ranting at me, 'Now you know what it's like, I told you!'

We set sail in a force six which I wouldn't even give a second thought to today, but to a lad who'd only ever been out in small day boats catching mackerel, this was a dramatic change to the big time. She rolled around and pitched like a bloated bath tub. The butterflies of excitement in my stomach turned into maggots of seasickness. This young Roger, who had put so much effort into persuading big bruv' to let him go to sea, now used all his energy longing for the calm of the harbour.

I spent the next four days lying behind the wheelhouse curled up in a pathetic ball waiting for the world to end. I couldn't have cared less if I'd been swept overboard; in fact I can remember hoping the boat would sink and that we'd all be drowned so that at least it would be over with. Nobody took a blind bit of notice of me except to kick or push me as they went past: a flea-ridden dog would have been treated better. I didn't care about anything except wanting to go home. Every time I tried to get up and move around the ship I only felt worse.

After four days I came to slightly and was rewarded by hearing Frank order me down into the fish hold. I was made to chop ice from the large blocks into the flakes used to pack the fish in the fish pounds. Down there, literally freezing, with the pitching and yawing of the boat accentuated and the smell of disinfectant mingling with the stench of old fish and diesel, I thought my time had come. The old Bible-bashing preachers had painted a frightening picture of a terrible hot, fiery place where sinners would go, but they were fairytales compared with this real, cold hell. I pleaded to be let up on deck, but Frank said that I'd wanted to come out and I was going to stick at it. The work was so physically demanding then and the hours so long, they had to be tough or there wouldn't have been any point in leaving the harbour.

I don't think the skipper, Wally Turrell, gave me more than a look. They were a breed apart, those skippers, hard men who would never speak to the crew, but only communicate through the mate. The only time the crew heard how they spoke would be when they got a tongue-lashing, which would usually go hand in hand with a physical beating. They expected far higher standards than the younger breed of skippers today. There was an incident of a North Sea skipper who was so disgruntled that his fish wasn't fried correctly that he came aft and put the cabin boy's hands into the hot frying fat. Mind you he was put in jail for it.

When we returned to Newlyn my Old Man asked, 'How d'you get on?'

'Well . . .' I didn't have to say any more.

'I knew that would happen!' He just shook his head sadly and carried on working at the lines on his small boat.

I said I was never going on a trawler again, particularly with brother Frank, although I was quite happy to go out in the bay.

But by Christmas I was back out again and gradually I overcame the sickness. I even went out with Brother again, going to sea during the holidays until I left school at fifteen.

All the youngsters served an apprenticeship at the net store in Newlyn, learning how to make up the gear, splice steel wire, and put a trawl together. Then we were let loose on the high seas.

During my first twelve months at sea full time, things improved. But painfully slowly. I felt squeamish every trip, and the tightening in my stomach every time I knew it was time to go below to chop ice took a long time to disappear. One aspect of life on board ship was guaranteed to make me feel bad again: the tea. I'd been used to having nice fresh milk at home, but this was before the days of UHT cartons, so we had to use condensed milk at sea. On that first boat there was a huge great teapot, and everything went into it: tea leaves, water, five or six great spoonfuls of sugar and the condensed milk. The whole mash was left to stew until it was a thick dark brown colour. It was so strong that the insides of all the tea cups were completely brown from the concentrated tannin. To make matters worse Frank would call me into the wheel-house to roll up cigarettes for him. He knew I was in a bad way, but he'd still call me in, and I can tell you that when he lit up it turned my stomach something awful. By the end of a watch with him it was almost a relief to go down into the fish room. The deck was no happier place. Cowhides were used on the bottom of the nets to stop them being chafed to death on the seabed. When the nets came in it was my task to climb right inside to check for holes. The stench from these cowhides as they dried was unbelievable.

The crew all reacted differently to watching yet another youngster go through all this. Some would try to help, telling me not to drink tea or eat anything except dry toast, others would be flippin' horrible. I never worked out whether they were trying to deter me from going to sea because they'd had such a terrible time themselves when they started out, or whether they just did to you what they'd had done to them.

After every couple of days on shore it took a real effort to go back down that quay. There was an indescribable smell when you went into the galley after the boat had been closed up. The oilskins were always left hanging around the place, damp and covered with old bits of fish guts, giving off a terrible stench as they dried out. Things didn't get any better when the cabin stove was lit. The flue went up through the galley and was lagged with asbestos but still gave off a tremendous heat. The oilies were hung around this to dry and the smells increased. It was enough to make me heave.

Without today's satellite positioning system, radar and Decca navigators which tell us to within a hundred yards where we are in the world, the watchkeeper had more to do. The only method we had of finding our position, apart from sextants and dead reckoning, was by using simple radio direction-finding beacons which the Germans set up during the war for their bombers to use. They were known as 'pips and squeaks', and usually only the skippers and mates knew how to use them.

So most of the time we would simply steam for forty miles from the Longships lighthouse, measured by the spinning log we towed behind us, and drop a buoy with a light on it to mark a start position. Then we'd shoot the nets and steam away, making a square course back to the buoy. The members of the crew who hadn't learnt any navigation wouldn't get us lost, because all they had to do was keep the buoy in sight.

At night the buoy was lit by an old carbide light. We had no choice but to use them because the paraffin hurricane lights were not reliable enough, nor did they give out a strong light. When I started at sea it was my most hated job to light it – for a small lad already feeling nauseous it was pure hell. You had to take two or three little pieces of carbide out of the storage box, place them in the bottom of the lamp and fill a container above it with water. The water dripped slowly on to the carbide chips, producing a gas which was then ignited. The stink used to make me feel very bad. Even thinking about it here sitting under the clean odour-free electric light of my cabin, I can feel that gas attacking me.

There was a terrible game that some of the older boys used to play, which I hated watching. They would take a piece of the carbide, stuff it into the mouth of a small fish, which they'd throw overboard for a seagull to gulp down. As soon as the carbide started to react with the water in the bird's stomach, it would produce the gas. Before long you'd see a puff of feathers as the poor bird disintegrated from the pressure.

Feelings of seasickness are impossible to describe and the movement in trawlers is the worst kind. Andrew Munson, the harbour master in Newlyn, gave up fishing because he couldn't get over his seasickness. He was telling me that it's been proved that people who suffer from seasickness are normal, and those who don't are abnormal, because the body *should* get confused by the movement at sea. I can tell you I was very normal. I don't think there are any magic cures except experience, but suddenly and mercifully it was as though I'd never had any problem at all.

I was really too young when I tried to get my mate's ticket, so I had to appear before the instructor to obtain dispensation to act as mate. I went to Falmouth with two others from Newlyn who were much older and more experienced. When it came to the exams one had problems with colour blindness and the other didn't know what the compass rose on the charts was for. They were probably both better seamen than me, with a lifetime's fishing experience, but I was the only one to get my temporary ticket.

The first ship I was mate on was the *St Clair*, an ex-naval supply ship built in the 1940s for carrying food supplies out to the big ships, and designed to be turned into a fishing boat after the war. She'd arrived in Newlyn when I was eleven and I can remember thinking 'She's a big 'un.'

The *St Clair* was in great shape when she arrived in our port – the ultimate in size, condition and speed. I remember seeing her go to sea at high tide, in the dark, with all her lights blazing away. She was bigger, more powerful and better kitted out than anything else out of Newlyn.

In 1961 the mate left her and I was asked to take his place. There was an intense rivalry between the youngsters then: who could mend nets fastest or splice a rope quickest. The word soon went around who was good and I was chuffed to be considered the best. As a seventeen-year-old it was an amazing honour to be asked to be the mate on the biggest ship in the port, the finest in the fleet. I was so proud.

Mitch's dad was aboard her; Jiggy was cook. Archie Swan, the father of our current shore engineer, was mechanic. We were top notchers. She was a beautiful craft fitted out just like a house; in fact we treated her better than our shore homes. Down in the sleeping quarters there was a coal stove with a plate on top for a kettle, and in winter my first duty on coming aboard was to light that stove. The ships were spotless then: you'd never see any dust, everything was polished, the wooden deck was scrubbed white with chloride of lime to kill the green algae. Even the forepeak where all the odds and ends were kept was immaculate, so much so that any of the crew could go down there in the dark and find exactly what they wanted without fear of falling over a pile of rubbish. Today on most ships you'd break your neck trying to do the same. I've known us to come home in a force seven or eight, scrubbing the inside of the remotest corners of the ship, obscure places you couldn't even see.

There was generally a lot more to do on the boats in those days. We'd spend two or three days awake at a time, mending gear and keeping everything in top condition. Despite that dreadful leaden heaviness after you've been awake for seventy-two hours, nobody really minded too much because you were busy and you knew it was all part of keeping up a high standard. There was a genuine pride taken in all we did.

Three and a half years after I'd gone as mate, I injured my hand and was forced to stay ashore with a poisoned finger. I was getting seven pounds six shillings a week sick money, so I decided I might as well use the time to go up to Plymouth and try for my ticket which would allow me to take a boat as skipper. You were supposed to spend four years at sea as a mate before you could study again but I was allowed to take the course and make up my sea time afterwards. We were taught very hard, to the extent that we were convinced we'd never get through the exam, but when it arrived it was so relatively easy we were sure there was something wrong. We all passed and could then act as skipper on any boat up to fifty tons, and also as mate on a steam trawler, which wasn't particularly useful since they'd all gone!

I hadn't long got my ticket when Newlyn was hit by a strike. The lorry drivers wanted all the shore staff to join their union, as they had done in the other ports. All lorries were prevented from coming into Newlyn which meant we couldn't get fuel, or send the fish off. After a while Old Man Willie Stevenson and his sons, who are now my bosses, overcame this by converting one of the trawlers into a fuel tanker, and by using another to export the fish straight across to France. But when it all started no one was sure whether or not they'd be able to sell any fish. I'd been living on sick money for weeks and I needed to earn some cash, so I decided to go off to Lowestoft as a mate. What I saw there convinced me that heavy unionization would be a disaster for Newlyn.

As mate I was in charge of the fish room, keeping track of what we'd caught, and organizing the unloading of the fish which, in Lowestoft, included filling in a landing form stating how many boxes you had. One day I was called into the harbour office, where a man called Cappy Hammond told me in no uncertain terms that I was to be careful. I'd been used to giving them a rough idea in Newlyn – some days you'd be over, others under, in the end it all evened out. Up there if you weren't within a couple of boxes the union would refuse to unload your ship again.

I came home to Newlyn as often as I could. Before one trip, my girlfriend Joan said to me that if we caught a small halibut I was to bring it home. But we didn't catch anything smaller than about six foot long by one and a half feet thick, so I found the smallest of these monsters and kept it down in the fish room.

I came home on the train carrying it in the only thing I could find which was large enough, a pillow-case. When I arrived in London I found I had to wait until the one o'clock sleeper, so I had a few hours to kill. There was no way I was going around the city with the pillow-case slung over my shoulder, so I had a bit of a think. Then I saw the left luggage lockers on the platform and stuffed the pillow-case, with its six-foot fish, into one at the top.

I went off to town, had a few drinks and a general look around before returning to the station later than I'd intended. As I rushed to the left luggage lockers I noticed that a tiny trickle of red was making its way down the doors. With horror I realized what had happened. The blood (which had congealed and frozen after the halibut had been gutted and put in the ice room) had melted. I opened the locker door very cautiously and sure enough the pillow-case was sitting on a pool of blood. I looked around to see if anyone had noticed, but there weren't that many people in the station. Slightly confused by alcohol, I thought, hell, what am I going to do now. The train was about to leave and I didn't want to be held up by any sort of challenge from a nosey passer-by. So I took my jacket off, wrapped the bleeding pillow-case in it and stumbled for the platform, leaving behind a steady trickle of blood.

All the way along the platform I waited for the shout, but, relieved and surprised, I made the train without having my collar felt. I asked the guard to put my package somewhere cool, and it arrived home safely where everyone had a little piece at a great feast. But the enjoyment was spoilt for me because I spent the next few days scouring the papers, convinced that I would read about a police search being started after the discovery of unidentifiable blood in a luggage locker at Paddington station. Whenever I went through Paddington after that I broke out in a cold sweat, afraid to look over my shoulder, just waiting to be arrested.

I got friendly with lots of men up in Lowestoft, even Cappy Hammond who'd made my life difficult. He told me a story of how he used to go off doing relief trips as skipper and was on board one ship to let the usual skipper go off on holiday with his wife and two kids. Cappy woke up one morning and looked across at the chart table, which was alongside the berth in the skipper's cabin, and he saw the bloke he'd relieved standing there looking at the charts. He turned out and went into the wheelhouse where he said to the watchkeeper that he'd just seen their skipper in his cabin. An hour later they had a link call on the radio from the shore to tell them that the skipper had dived into the shallow end of a swimming pool, broken his neck and had just died. If that isn't spine-tingling I don't know what is.

The strike in Newlyn soon ended. There are no unions on the quayside. I was off on my career as a skipper.

I started work for the Stevensons' company as they moved into trawling. Up until that point, most of the local Newlyn boats had been pilchard drifting or long lining, using simple nets or long lines of hooks to catch surface-feeding fish, like pilchards, mackerel or herring. Every year the Lowestoft fishermen came down around the Isles of Scilly shooting nets for mackerel. Then later in the season they would swop the drift nets for trawls, to target the bottom-feeding fish such as sole. They'd come from a town which had its own school for skippers, so they had all the latest know-how about trawling. They also knew how to attract the local females and many ended up marrying Newlyn girls and staying.

Seeing how successful the Lowestoft lads were at trawling, Willie Stevenson decided to convert one of his boats and employ a Lowestoft skipper. It worked out well.

After the war all the navy's Motor Fishing Vessels which had been used for running supplies were decommissioned, so Old Man Willie decided to build up a fleet of trawlers using these ships. But none of the old Newlyn skippers had the right experience and weren't really interested in changing over from netting or lining anyway. So before too long nearly three-quarters of the skippers here were Lowestoft men.

It was a time of change. Old Man Willie handed over to his sons: Billy ran the boats, Tony the fish selling, and we were the first generation of locals to be trained up specifically to work trawlers.

I was twenty-two and working as mate when Billy came over to me wringing his hands, which is a habit of his, and mumbled, 'You can have the trawler *William* for a week. I know you won't do any good, but have a go anyhow,' then wandered off. I couldn't believe it. Normally you waited for years and years to step into dead men's shoes, but out of the blue I'd become a skipper, joining all the old boys I'd always looked up to.

It was an exhilarating and terrifying prospect. When you're mate you know that if anything happens the old man's behind you

OVERLEAF Longships Lighthouse, off Land's End

to leap in and take over. If you have a bad trip and don't land much fish then it isn't your fault. As skipper you're the one in charge, the one with all the responsibility: on the other hand when you do get a good trip there's nothing like it. The prospect delighted and frightened me at the same time.

Two years ago when Ernie Hunter died I became the longest serving skipper in Newlyn, which makes me feel very old.

And now it's all changing again. A new generation of the Stevenson family are taking over the business. Will there also be a new type of fishing to revitalize the industry, or will it come to a complete stop as it has in other ports up and down the country? The costs of the gear, the amount of interest on loans and all the restrictions on what we can catch where don't encourage young-sters to look at fishing favourably, knowing it will be difficult for them to make a living at it. Today we're like hunters who've been blindfolded and had their hands tied behind their backs.

Sitting out here as we approach the time to give the lads a shout to shoot the trawls, I can't help thinking back to the excitement I felt as a small boy when I couldn't wait for the day I would go to sea. That excitement seems to have turned to apathy in what should be the next generation of fishermen.

Shooting the trawls

56

 TODAY'S BEEN ONE of those beautiful clear spring days with not a trace of wind, and a flat calm, glassy sea. The sky's deep blue, the intense cold has gone and there's even a suggestion that winter might be over. The warps towing the nets along cut through the oily water with hardly more than a gentle ripple. All the doors and windows have been flung open to let the crisp air in, and I even thought I heard Tony humming as he went down into the fish hold to collect the food for tonight's meal.

I've been sitting out on the afterdeck smoking, and as your mind blocks out the roar of the engine it almost seems peaceful out here. I'd even go as far as to say there's nowhere I'd rather be. It's difficult to imagine that there's ever any danger out here at all.

We passed another trawler, *Pietre J*, whose crew were out on deck sunning themselves. Years ago she was one of the finest boats I skippered and the one from which I nearly lost my first man.

I was in my bunk when the engineer came up shouting, 'Quick, quick, we've lost Perry!' I leapt out, ran to the wheelhouse, and by sheer fluke saw him in the water behind us, disappearing rapidly. A deep swell was running and I knew I had to keep my eyes on him because once you lose sight of a man overboard in those conditions you never find him again.

The mate turned the boat around towards the direction of my outstretched arm, being careful not to run Perry down in the process. I can't imagine anything worse than the water level view of a huge trawler bearing down on you, so although speed is important, care and accuracy are vital. We came alongside Perry, grabbed his arms and held him against the side of the boat, just keeping very calm and not making any big deal out of it. After a few moments to let him get his breath back we pulled him on board, took him aft and put him under a warm shower.

In the galley over a mug of tea we heard what had happened. All hands had been on the deck shooting the nets as we do every four hours or so around the clock. Just as the nets slipped over the side Perry had caught his foot in the rope which is tied to the bottom of the net and he'd been swept overboard. Snared by his ankle he'd been dragged along under the water at four or five knots. It must have been terrifying. Even though the net had only just gone over the side he must have been about eighteen feet under the surface. The force as he was pulled through the water was so

great that he was streamed out like a waterskier, being towed along by his foot, with his hands trailing behind his head. All he could see above him was a mass of air bubbles from the net being dragged through the water. He thought that was it, but by forcing himself to do a sort of sit-up against the current he managed to grab hold of his clothes and pull his arms down his body and along his leg. He must have been very strong, because he managed to pull himself up until he was bent double, and could reach his foot, all the time straining against the force of the water. By one of those lucky breaks, he was wearing my seaboots which were a size too big for him. As soon as he released the tension from the rope he was able to wriggle his foot out. Then he was free and bobbed to the surface.

All this happened in the space of about a couple of minutes. Perry said that by the end his lungs were bursting and he knew he couldn't have held out for much longer before he would have been forced to take a lungful of water.

When he reached the surface he saw the boat disappearing, and was sure that we'd not even seen him go over. The relief when we turned back towards him must have been wonderful. Perry was none the worse for his dunking and was back on the deck working within the hour.

It was a damn good job he could swim. I don't know how fishermen can stand being out here if they can't. I've watched Mitch's sixteen stone clamber out to the end of derrick forty feet from the *William Sampson*'s side to work on the gear, and wondered how we'd manage if he went in. He can't swim a stroke and I don't know how he copes with it. I've seen several men go over the side in far less dodgy circumstances.

I once worked on a boat which was using lines to catch turbot. You shoot just as daylight is coming, then leave the lines there until about one o'clock when the sun's overhead and pull them in. When you get a male turbot on the hook, two or three free-swimming females will follow him up from the seabed right up to the side of the boat where they'll swim across the surface around him. It's quite sad to see really. The skipper, Kenny Downing, would be there with a gaff hook ready to spear these loose females. He was so keen to get every last fish that one day he overreached and fell right in, boots and all. I can see him there in the water

---

PREVIOUS PAGES Another trawler from the Newlyn fleet

hanging on to the gaff hook, treading water while we laughed ourselves stupid. He was slightly more careful after that.

We've not always been able to retrieve men overboard. We had a Polish chap, Jan Lozinski, on board a few years back, an interesting man who'd been maltreated by the Germans during the war when they kept him locked in a small crate. He'd never really recovered from the ordeal physically or mentally and had spent long periods of time off work, under treatment from the doctor. He decided to come back to sea at a time when I was looking for a deckhand for a trip, so I said I'd take him. We picked him up at five o'clock in the morning and steamed off. I was in the wheelhouse, the lads were aft in the galley eating, and he'd said he was feeling a bit queasy so had gone out on the afterdeck with his sandwiches for some fresh air.

When he didn't return after about an hour one of the lads thought he ought to have a look to see if Jan was all right.

The wrapper from his sandwiches was there on the deck, but there was no other sign of him. We turned the ship around to search for him, and other boats joined us to sweep the area. At one point we saw a flock of seagulls hovering above the water for no apparent reason and I thought they might have been feeding on his sandwiches, but we found nothing. It was as though he'd been whisked away by aliens. We could only imagine that he'd been seasick and in the process of hanging over the side he'd lost his balance and fallen in.

We steamed back into harbour and I had to go up to the house to tell his wife and children the bad news. They were all in the front room sitting by the fire along with Jan's dog, and it was as though that animal knew his master had gone. It looked up at me as I entered the room, then before I said anything just hung its head and ambled away dejectedly. The image of that pathetic dog has stayed with me more than the reactions of the people, it was such an instinctive action by the poor animal. Jan became another name to add to all the others lost at sea.

EARLY THIS MORNING my few minutes' peace in the galley with my *Fishing News* crossword was disturbed by Jiggy's manic cackle over the intercom from the bridge. 'Your friend's here, Roger!' he sang. I raced out on to the deck as the twin-engined Dornier swooped low over the boat.

The plane is as unwelcome to us as a dead albatross was to the Ancient Mariner. It's one of the Ministry of Agriculture, Fisheries and Food (MAFF) spotter planes which fly over British fishing grounds, recording the positions, names and numbers of all fishing boats. They pass them on to the naval vessels which police the 200 mile territorial waters, targeting any boats which look as though they're up to no good.

The regulations are complex and constantly changing, but the main ones are that boats need licences to fish in British waters, and within them can only work in certain areas depending on their type of gear, boat length and engine power. The *William Sampson* is a large beam trawler with an engine over 800 horsepower and trawl beams eight metres long, so we're only supposed to work outside a twelve mile limit. There are also restrictions on what fish we're allowed to catch. The details are based on a complicated system of quotas per boat for quantity of each species caught in the different sea areas, restrictions on the size of net meshes, and a minimum size for each type of fish. Confused? Well so are we! There are more and more rules to obey each week. Last time I was in the local MAFF office in Newlyn they showed me the large blue book containing all the up to date regulations for fishing around British waters. God managed to get all his rules for the world on a stone tablet, MAFF would have needed a whole quarry's worth.

Sure enough a couple of hours after the plane had disappeared we saw the grey shape of one of Her Majesty's minesweepers appear over the horizon. I thought she was heading for us, but she turned and moved towards a Belgian beamer over on our starboard bow. A tiny fleck of orange was lowered over the minesweeper's side and the inflatable boat with the two boarding officers went across to inspect the trawler. There are something like seven naval boats out on fisheries protection duties, and we've had the pleasure of the company of most of them at one time or another. We're convinced the *William Sampson* has a homing device on her mast.

Jiggy was on watch, the rest were turned in, and I went below to the galley to get myself another coffee. Jiggy's whistle over the intercom summoned me back to the wheelhouse in time to hear the repeated radio message.

'*William Sampson*, this is Fisheries patrol vessel *Sheraton*, channel 77 please.' Jiggy turned the VHF radio set to channel 77 and I replied.

'*Sheraton*, this is *William Sampson*. What can I do for you?' I hoped they were just bored and wanted to pass the time of day while they were waiting for their boarding party to return.

'Good morning to you, Skipper, just a few questions if I may.' It feels just like being stopped in your car and questioned by the police. You keep wondering if that tyre on the back wheel is still just legal, or if they'll notice that your rear brake light isn't working. The difference is that these fishing rules are twenty times more precise and complicated than the highway code.

After a few preliminary enquiries about how long we'd been at sea, and what we'd caught, the dreaded words came over.

'OK, Skipper, I'd like to send a couple of my chaps over to you. They'll be about five minutes. Please leave your nets down until they're on board.'

Jiggy let out one of his cackling laughs. 'We're in for it now, boys.'

If you speak to any of the other skippers or crews in any fishing port in the country you'll hear tales of how this request to board can create instant havoc. Even if you think you're fishing within the law you're always slightly nervous. You never know if you may have accidentally broken one of the hundreds of rules.

A few years ago we were told we were to be boarded and I knew I had some boxes of cod in the fish hold. Unfortunately there was a total ban on catching cod at the time. There was nothing for it: I called the lads out and turned the boat away from the naval vessel so that the boys could scurry along the blind side to the fish hold, climb down below and pass the cod up on deck so it could be dumped over the side. It was ridiculous really, the naval ship couldn't have failed to see a trail of dead, gutted cod floating mysteriously away from us in a long line. When we were boarded the officer went through the catch and asked how much cod we had. Feeling smug I told him that we hadn't any. Trying not to smile the officer said, 'So you haven't used any of your quota, then?' I couldn't believe it – the rules had changed while we'd been at sea, and I'd just thrown several hundred pounds' worth of hard work over the side for no reason.

To be honest we've been forced to become a bit like poachers just to catch enough to make a living. There aren't many fishermen who haven't gone a bit over a quota, or fished slightly inside the twelve mile limit on occasions. For once, though, I was sure that we'd not been up to anything we shouldn't have been today.

The inflatable came shooting across to us and the two officers in their orange immersion suits climbed on board. It's not too difficult an operation on our boat because they only have to climb a few feet over the rail. On some of the large French stern trawlers or Spanish long liners they have to leap across at a rope ladder and climb twenty or thirty feet up the side of a rolling ship, with a deep swell rising and falling beneath them. Not something I would want to attempt four or five times a day.

The First Lieutenant and the Chief Petty Officer were pleasant enough as they went through the standard routine – most of them are. Having checked the log book and licence details they asked me to haul the nets. This can be one of the nail-biting parts. They have to measure the size of the mesh at the cod end, the narrow part of the nets where the fish are actually trapped, and look for blinders which used to be a widespread illegal practice. They were nets within the net which had a smaller mesh designed to catch under-size fish. They're very difficult to detect unless you're on board, and the idea is to be able to jettison the blinder easily so that you end up with an innocent set of gear. In the area we're fishing in at the moment I was sure the regulation minimum was eighty-five millimetres and we weren't towing a blinder.

Naval boarding party

The boarding officer started taking the ten readings with the triangular gauge and his number two noted them down to calculate the average. From the wheelhouse I heard the sizes being called out. To my alarm there seemed to be quite a few seventy-nines in there. Time to light a roll-up. When the second officer pressed the button on his calculator and shouted 'Average, eighty point three.' I thought we were in real trouble. I swung down the ladder on to the deck ready to make excuses. As casually as I could I started to tell them how we'd been picking up lots of sand in that net which might have tightened the mesh slightly.

'Yes, you'll have to watch it. It was a bit close there in places.' I couldn't believe it; I was convinced I was on my way to prison.

'It's eighty-five here, isn't it?' I asked casually.

'No, eighty millimetres,' he replied. I was a very relieved man.

There was one similar occasion when the nets really had been undersized and I'd told the officer he wasn't pushing the measure into the mesh hard enough, because when I took the ten readings on the same meshes they were a lot bigger. He'd asked me if I was going to argue with him in which case we could easily go back into port and get a ruling. We came to a compromise: I cut the nets off in front of him and put two new ones on.

There's a fairly healthy mutual respect between the navy and the fishermen. After all, we're all out here at sea doing a job and we both know what hell it can be. On the other hand I don't have quite the same respect for the way their masters treat us. It seems to me that more and more is being put in our way to stop us from getting on with the fishing. British boats seem to be tied down by regulations, while other countries are allowed to get away with breaking the rules. If we're found to be fishing illegally for any of the variety of reasons we have to report to the local MAFF office, while in principle foreign boats are escorted back to the nearest British port where they're prosecuted in a magistrates' court within twenty-four hours.

For all the regulations, however, there don't seem to be many actual arrests of foreign boats, and MAFF seem to be more afraid of causing an international incident than policing the regulations. Only the other day a flag of convenience Spaniard, with English skipper, mate and registration, but Spanish crew and owner, was boarded and found to be without a licence, but then let go. There are countless boats out there breaking the rules, especially foreign ones. We know that many Spanish and Belgian boats have false compartments on board to store illegal fish, and yet the navy never seems to find them. They always claim that there are no such things but I've been on board some of these ships and been shown hidden holds, down in the bilges or behind lockers. Mitch was a mate on a Spaniard, and, although they kept him in the dark for much of the time, he eventually discovered their illegal hold.

It's all a farce, really. Even if they don't hide fish, most fishing boats falsify their log books. They say they're catching fish where they're not, and change one fish species to another. The terrible thing is that the scientists who are deciding what we can catch where, are using this false information to decide the very con- straints that we then spend the next trip trying to avoid. Their picture of what's really going on in the sea must be complete rubbish. It's not a practice I like getting involved in, but as soon as one person starts it everyone else has to join in to survive. They're talking about bringing in some sort of satellite tracking system for boats like they have for aircraft. Each boat would send out a callsign which would then show up on a map in some master control room. Until that happens the ministry's naval operation which costs around £6,500,000 every year can only monitor a few boats, and, frankly, unless you're seen by the navy or the plane you can say what you like in your log book.

There's a lot of fiddling, too, once the catch is ashore. It's easy to land a little bit more fish than we're supposed to round the back of the market, black fish as it's called. There was a case in Lowestoft only last week where a ship was fined for just that.

Maybe we do need these gamekeepers. After all, I'm sure there's something of a poacher in all fishermen, who are really the last of the hunters.

I suppose we were brought up to think of poaching as a bit of a laugh. When I was in my teens we used to go out hunting rabbits on a farmer's private land just outside Newlyn. I enjoyed nothing better than the nights when the old boy would turn up and start shooting at us. Admittedly it was always well over our heads, but the rush of adrenalin was thrilling. Brother Frank used to wear a pair of long thigh waders to go into the mud where he'd often get bogged down and stuck when the farmer turned up. I'd hear him shout, 'Wait for me, Bro', and I'd shout back in no uncertain terms that he could fend for himself. I was off.

Even now when I hear stories of the salmon poachers up on the River Camel something stirs in me. They must have great fun some nights with the water bailiffs out looking out for them, while they're safely holed up in some small creek hiding under the shelter of the overhanging trees or behind a rock. To be quite truthful I imagine it's not a great deal different from fishing slightly inside the limit on one of these trawlers. You're alert, watching and waiting to sight the naval patrol, ready to make a run for it.

Time ticked by this morning as the MAFF inspection continued. Down in the hold they measured the fish we had on board to check for undersized samples. They also look for any quantities above the quota for each species or evidence of any types of fish which are totally banned at the moment. The Spanish are keen on catching undersize megrim, as there's a great trade in them for drying and salting. On the whole British boats don't bother because they don't get good prices here, so it's not worth the risk.

We did have a problem a few weeks ago on the market in Newlyn when we were found to have just fifteen soles slightly undersize. We'd had a youngster on board who wasn't used to measuring the fish, and he'd let these few slip through, out of thousands. We were told that if we were caught again we'd be in serious trouble. That doesn't seem to match up to the case in Milford Haven where a Spanish flag of convenience trawler was caught with 150 boxes of undersize fish hidden on board, and fined just £4500. He'd had engine trouble, and radioed in to say that he needed to go into Milford Haven for help, but wanted to land his fish in Pembroke which was further away. Now there isn't a MAFF office in Pembroke; there was however a keen young MAFF man who thought it all sounded odd. He went across and discovered a secret fish room hidden behind a wall of ice, holding eight tons of undersize fish. When you consider that lot would have been worth around £12,000 on the Spanish market, the fine was worth risking. I don't feel you can blame the Spanish fishermen for doing this while their own government lets them get away with it, but it doesn't seem right that we were threatened over a handful of accidentally kept soles compared with that deliberate attempt at deception.

The whole process is a mess. When you're bringing up fish from 200 fathoms the small megrim are dead anyway, so there doesn't seem any point in throwing them back if they can be sold. In the same way we're on a limit for cod at the moment, and if we catch a full size cod when we're over that we're supposed to throw it back, even if it's dead. Can't be right, can it?

There wasn't much fish in our hold for the navy boys to see today, since this was only the fourth catch of our trip. The rest of our log books and records tallied with what they'd seen so they were happy. They gave me their ship's badge to add to the five we have stuck up on the side of the radio in the wheelhouse. Only one more to go before we could claim our bottle of whisky from the navy. The inflatable returned to HMS *Sheraton* with a trophy from us in return, a bag of fish for the thirty or so men on board.

The regulations have become such a part of our lives out here that they feature in my recurring dream. It all happens in the harbour in the days before the new quay was built, when there was a huge mudbank there. I'm in a ship trawling, and I've got to act drastically to avoid the mudbank. I've got the wheel hard over and I'm leaning out of the window pulling her around. Can I get her around before I hit the engineer's hut, and without turning the trawl over? It's a tense few moments watching her bow and wondering if she'll miss the old pier. But I always make it around and think, 'Well that's all right, but I'm going to have to haul the gear now,' and I think to myself, 'I'm inside the limit, so I'll have to haul in the dark, very quietly.' I can see all the lights on the shore, I'm so close I can even see people leaving the pubs and I think to myself that they can't see me because I'm all in the dark. Eventually I get the nets in and usually it's a good catch as well.

I often ring my wife Nellie up in the morning and say to her, 'I've been in the harbour fishing again last night.' I'm not the only one who dreams he's fishing in the harbour either. I suppose it's my worst nightmare of being caught as far inside the limit as it's possible to be!

I was talking on the radio to Brother one evening and he was going on about how good the fishing was where he was. I knew that he wasn't anywhere near the position he said he was, but in fact he was inside the twelve mile limit because I'd seen him. So I decided to get my own back on him for trying to give me false information.

I took one of the white scallop storage bags out of the hold, stretched it across the galley table and turned it into a White Ensign – as flown by the Royal Navy – using coloured insulating tape. We tied it to the top of our mast, then waited until dusk and steamed towards him. By the time we reached him it was a dark moonless night, just the right conditions for carrying out under-cover sorties. After we'd made sure there were no other boats around, I got the boys to black out the ship and put up a new white light over the wheelhouse. In the dark, through binoculars, it would be hard to make out our shape, and with only the navigational lights showing we would have looked just like a naval ship.

We moved close to Brother like this just as the navy boys do, but he didn't spot us until we got close, and I shone the Aldis signalling lamp on the makeshift White Ensign. Through my binoculars I could see Brother in the wheelhouse as he spotted what he thought was the navy and I could almost see the panic. It was like watching a silent movie. He shouted orders down to his men who were aft having their meal. Next thing, out went his green and white fishing lights and on came two red lights up his mast which is the international signal indicating that the boat is no longer under command. I nearly fell off my wheelhouse chair laughing because I knew it was just the sort of daft thing I would do if I were caught in the same way. I could imagine Frank thinking, 'I'll fool these bright young naval officers into thinking that I'm not fishing and in fact I've lost any ability to steer the boat, which is why I'm inside the limit.'

Then we saw movement on deck as the crew ran forward trying to keep out of sight. They were going to attempt to bring in the nets without the naval ship seeing them, but the winch was on deck so Brother had to get all the men out there to operate it, a complete giveaway to start with. All this time he kept turning the boat away from us to try and give his men cover, but I just gave my boat a boost and kept pace with him, copying his moves. One lad on board with Brother, Lowestoft Bob, was seventeen stone and a big chap. He was struggling with the others to keep out of sight, all working away on their hands and knees, and he told us in the pub afterwards that all the time Frank was screaming, 'The navy's here! Get out on the decks, pull the trawls in and we'll jam the brakes on and say we were having problems!'

We got closer and closer, laughing until it hurt at the panicked cover-up attempt. In the end we were so close that his deck lights picked out our shape. As it dawned on him what had happened Frank shouted at me using every term of abuse he could think of.

He tried to say that he'd known it was me. But I took great satisfaction in knowing that he'd been caught good and proper.

I came back into port with the ensign still streaming from our mast. Our boss Billy Stevenson asked me what the flag was for, and I told him. 'I've been on fisheries patrol!'

OVERLEAF With Brother Frank on the quay at Newlyn

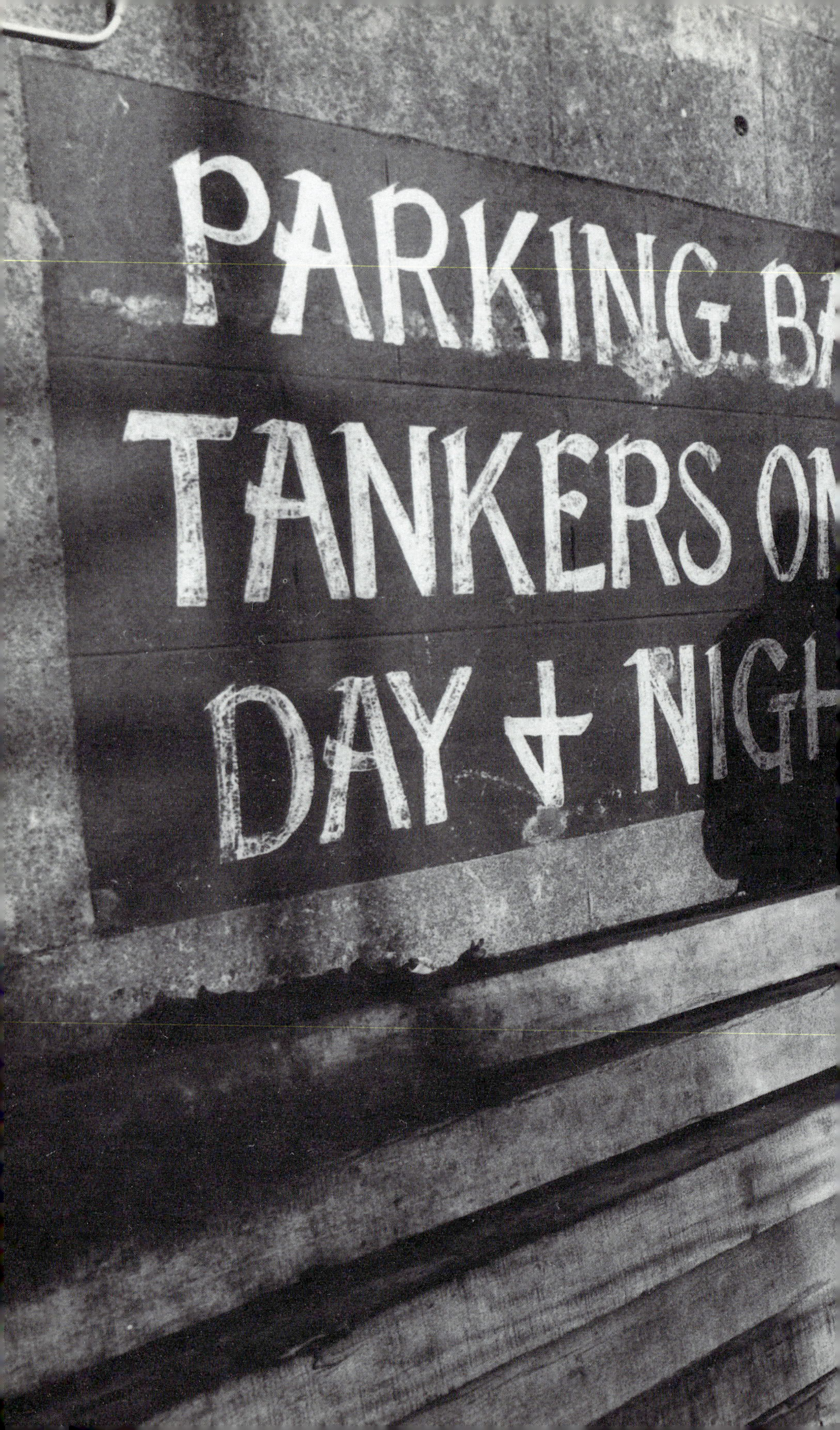
PARKING BA
TANKERS ON
DAY + NIGH

I'VE JUST COME back to sea after a couple of days off. It started well when the three of us, Nell, Sophie and I, went over to watch the traditional Helston Furry dance, the one with the song that Terry Wogan ruined a few years back. I'd never been to the dance in all my years, but Sophie and Nellie wanted to go. I was all in but I couldn't say no, especially after the letter Sophie had given me when I arrived home. She'd addressed it to 'Daddy, on boat William Stevenson, North Sea'. She said, 'I couldn't post it because the postman wouldn't have known where you were.' How could I resist her? She winds me round her little finger so easily. The letter had a picture of her dancing and told me how she'd learnt to do the splits. It made me realize that she's growing up fast, and I've missed most of her six years.

That was probably on my mind over at Helston when I met John Wannell, a bloke I used to fish with but haven't seen for years. In between the two town bands, as all the dancers in their morning suits and posh frocks passed us, he told me that he's been ashore for a year now. He was fed up with fishing and wanted to see more of his family. It always makes me laugh when you hear of politicians retiring to spend more time with their families – they see a damn sight more of them than we do of ours. John said it had taken twelve months for his children to turn round and ask him to do something rather than their mother, they were so unused to having him around.

He said he'd discovered for the first time what it was like to have a family other than the men on the boat. He's right, for all your working life the crew on board are more of a family than your real family ashore. You spend more time with them, in far closer circumstances than most men do with their wives.

Nellie had been watching the dance, but obviously listening to our conversation as well, because she turned and said with great feeling, 'We're worse than ships that pass in the night, you and me, Rog.'

Somehow it wasn't so bad when you could walk down the quay and know every single person and most likely their parents as well, and know that they were in the same situation. The village used to be like one big family, complete with its tiffs and quarrels, but on the whole supportive because most people ashore understood what our lives were like. This wasn't always a good thing –

in fact I moved out of the village because I began to find the atmosphere claustrophobic. It's all changed and today there are more and more strangers.

I found myself in a thoughtful mood right up until it was time to leave the house to come back to the boat this morning. Then Nellie dropped a bombshell. 'You had a visitor while you were at sea last week.' She didn't want to tell me who it was and I couldn't guess. In the end she admitted that it was a chap from the tax office, with a file under his arm which must be pretty thick by now, I should think.

At home with Nell and Sophie

We've been having discussions for years on and off, but lately it's gone very quiet. The last time someone contacted me in person was four years ago. There are piles of brown On Her Majesty's Service envelopes around the house, but I've given up opening them – they're too depressing. Nell told him I was at sea and he said he'd come again on Monday. But as it turns out here I am back out at sea again. And so it goes on.

There are more fishermen with tax problems than you could ever imagine. It's partly because of erratic earnings which are assessed at well above what you actually take home; partly because we're not known to be the best savers, and mostly down to an attitude of 'while you've got it spend it'.

My trouble really started several years ago when the boat had a two month lay-up and there was no money coming in. Everything we'd been saving to pay the tax was spent on keeping the mortgage going and we've never really recovered. I've told them I can't pay, but they just keep putting penalties on top of penalties and I'm well and truly stuffed. Out of the £38,000 or so that I owe, the fines alone come to several thousand pounds. It doesn't really bother me too much; I'd just like to get it all sorted out. My only hope is that they'll make me bankrupt soon so that I can wipe the slate clean and start again, but I suppose we'll just have to continue this waiting game. I won't be the first on this boat, and I'm sure not the last.

I know it worries Nell more than it does me, but she finds it hard to judge the right time to talk about it. She doesn't want to tackle the subject as soon as I walk through the door, nor spoil a nice couple of days off, but equally it's not the best time when you're on the quay about to go off again for nine days. To be quite truthful it's quite good sometimes to be able to take this boat out of the harbour and leave all that behind.

BOBBY'S SMALL ROUND figure stood on the end of the quay watching us go through the gaps this morning. As we left the harbour at the start of another ten days' trawling he waved us on our way with his cap, and he didn't seem too unhappy to be ashore. A few weeks back we noticed he would sometimes stop sorting the fish or mending the nets on deck and grab hold of the side of the boat. When we quizzed him he admitted to feeling dizzy every so often, but being Bobby he dismissed it as nothing. We kept an eye on him from then until a couple of weeks ago when he keeled over completely as we were hauling the nets. Mitch had to carry him aft and put him down in his bunk. He had a couple of goes at getting up to work on deck, but in the end we took him back into port. He's been off sick since then: the doctors say that it's something to do with arthritis in his neck which is affecting a nerve that controls balance. It's down to all the wear and tear you get out here, I'm sure. We couldn't believe it when the doctor said to him that he should get a job ashore. I don't know whether he or she has looked at the papers recently, but we've got an unemployment problem down here second only to the north of England. At sixty-three, after a lifetime at sea, Bobby is hardly going to be the most attractive potential employee, is he? I'll miss the old boy if he doesn't come back. He and I spent hours in the wheelhouse talking.

We've kept his place on the boat, but being short-handed was becoming too much for the rest of us, so as a temporary measure we've had a new boy, Richard, on board for the last couple of trips. He comes from across the border in Plymouth, but he's a good lad in spite of that. There's always been a bit of suspicion about people from up north down here. There's an advert on the wall in the pub in Newlyn clipped from a mid-nineteenth-century Cornish paper, where someone is looking for a housekeeper, 'People from north of the Tamar need not apply.'

I was down in the galley talking to Richard after the first haul of his first trip when I noticed his finger was wrapped around with insulating tape. I hadn't been aware of any accident, but when I asked him about it he told me that he'd trapped his right index finger between the net and the pin which guides it over the side. With the weight of the whole net bearing down on the finger it could do nothing else but snap. You only had to look at the way

75

his nail now stuck out at right angles to the rest of the finger to see that it must have come apart. Yet he had said nothing, just carried on working. I persuaded him to let me bandage it up a bit more securely than he'd done with his insulating tape and we never heard a murmur from him all trip.

I had to laugh because on the same trip Mitch cut his left index finger mending a net and one evening the two of them sat next to each other eating away at great mounds of food with their opposite index fingers sticking out, covered in bandage.

When Richard got to the doctors they said they were going to have to break it again before they could put a pin through to set it straight. So he's decided not to bother about it. He'll fit in well with all the other fishermen who've got a finger or some other part of their body missing or modified. A fishing port wouldn't feel right without its collection of one armed skippers, and crew with legs, fingers or eyes missing. You'd need a full set of fingers to count the number of accidents happening every week out at sea, there's so much dangerous machinery and gear flying around on the rolling deck of a fishing boat, twenty-four hours a day.

About seven years ago I was sleeping happily when I was disturbed by a vicious shake. Even rising through the depths of slumber the urgency in the engineer's voice was unmistakable.

'Roger, Roger, get up quick. Mark's been hit in the face with a rope!' I jumped out of my bunk and climbed down into the galley. I was greeted by the sight of a bloody mass where Mark's face should have been. Forcing myself to sound lighthearted I asked, 'What have you been and done now then, Mark?' I'll never forget the eerie way in which he put out his hand and shook mine, just like a robot, so severe was his state of shock. He had good reason to be in shock as well. This good-looking nineteen-year-old's face had been stripped flat. Where his nose should have been was just a mass of red – it looked like he'd come off a battlefield.

While I bandaged up his head as best as possible – the ship was rising and falling like a fairground ride – the others told me how the accident had happened. A nylon rope had jammed around the winch and snapped, sending the end flying across the deck. The strands acted like a flail, taking Mark's nose clean off. It was as though he'd been swiped by a huge steel tiger's claw, or a set of cheese wires. Through the red mass of raw flesh around his eye sockets it was impossible to tell if he'd lost an eye.

Our position was about sixteen miles off the Isles of Scilly when all this happened, so I called Land's End radio and asked for the Scillies' lifeboat to be launched. After a brief discussion with the coastguard we worked out that since I could steam at twelve knots, we would almost be there by the time the lifeboat crew had been called out and the boat launched. So we brought the trawls aboard and steamed towards the islands with the throttle wide open.

The old girl leapt ahead like a destroyer, the water at her bow surging up like a tidal wave above the deep Atlantic swell. While we were steaming I went off on one of the most unusual hunts ever, in search of the nose. I thought that if I could find it, it could go down in the ice room. Not long before this accident had happened, an arm had been chopped off by a warp on another ship. They'd found the limb, embedded it in ice, and surgeons had been able to sew it back on. But I was not so lucky. The nose had either gone over the side or, more likely, had been minced into such small particles that it didn't exist any more.

As the skipper in these situations you know you've got to keep calm because everyone else is watching you to judge the reaction they should have. One wrong look or intonation can send a crew into panic.

When we arrived in the harbour the coxswain of the lifeboat, Matt Lethbridge, was waiting with a doctor. They leapt aboard and the doctor injected Mark with morphine. Matt took seconds to see where the controls were and told me to get off with Mark to the hospital. Matt is one of the finest, bravest seafarers you could ever hope to meet and taking the helm of a strange trawler was nothing for him.

At the small island hospital they stabilized Mark's condition and stitched his eyes, but they couldn't do any of the plastic surgery which was necessary, so he was flown back to the mainland. A fantastic operation was carried out on him, cutting the skin of his forehead in such a way that they could pull it down over his face and construct a new nose. A few months later he arrived back in Newlyn complete with a perfect nose, wanting to go back to sea. We took him out but only got as far as the Longships lighthouse when he couldn't take any more, so we had to sail back in with him.

This kind of accident is all too common on fishing boats. There was a chap on my brother Frank's boat who got his hand caught in one of the winches. He thought he was all right until he took his glove off to have a look at the damage and found he'd left the top of his fingers behind.

Danger is ever-present on these boats. Every piece of equipment is under such great strain when you're towing the trawl that no matter how often you check and replace suspect gear there's always the possibility of hidden metal fatigue. You only have to imagine a hundred foot boat with a massive engine towing against two huge anchors, twenty-four hours a day to begin to understand the terrible stresses and strains on the system.

We've had all sorts of near misses out here, with blocks breaking and large chunks of metal flying down into the deck, missing people by inches. There are very few in Newlyn who haven't lost a family member or one of their crew when some piece of gear has broken under strain. As long as all the equipment is maintained to the highest standard and changed as soon as you think it's getting even slightly dodgy then that's all you can do. You're always aware of the dangers and they're in the front of your mind even if you don't express them often.

We were towing along quietly one morning in a beautiful flat calm sea. All the lads were on deck including Wugg, a young deckhand who'd not long been with us. They were gutting the last few fish before hauling in the gear again when there was an almighty crack like an iron whip. I rushed to the starboard side of the wheelhouse and saw that one of the chains holding the derricks in position had parted. The derrick swung back in, scooped up Wugg's body across his midriff and slammed it on top of the winch. The force was so great that it left a huge crater where it then hit the wheelhouse.

We moved Wugg aft into the galley where we laid him on the table. He was a ghostly grey colour and wasn't moving, but despite the ferocity of the impact there was not a trace of blood or other evidence of damage anywhere on his body. We took it in turns to give him mouth to mouth resuscitation as we steamed back towards the Longships lighthouse off Land's End.

Before long we were convinced he was dead. There was absolutely no sign of life in the man, and by the time the lifeboat appeared we all felt helpless.

I'd been talking to him every so often in case he could still hear, and even though I knew things were desperate I kept up the chat. 'It's all right now, Wugg, the lads have arrived.' This man who should have been dead lifted his hand and put it under mine. It was a terrible shock, but suddenly there was hope.

When the lifeboat came alongside us I went up to the wheelhouse while the crew prepared to throw ropes across to lash the boats together. As we were tied together Padstow Pete called up, 'Roger!' and when I looked back he just shook his head slowly.

Dr Woods jumped aboard and had a look at him. He reassured us that nothing could have been done to save Wugg even if the accident had happened outside an operating theatre. Although there was no exterior evidence of damage, his spleen and liver had been completely smashed.

Inevitably the instant reaction on everyone's part was to relive the moment. The chap who'd been on the other side of the deck told me that Wugg had just finished bending over gutting the last fish and straightened up at the moment the chain parted. It's unbelievable how unlucky that kid was. Who knows what might have been if there'd been one more or one less fish. Pat, who was working next to him, had his hat knocked off and his forehead gashed. If Pat had been standing upright at that moment we could have lost two men.

We didn't have an autopilot in those days so I said to the doctor, a yachtsman, 'You steer.' While he took her along the coast and into the harbour I went aft with the boys and we tidied up Wugg's clothes and wiped away the tiny drop of blood that had now appeared around his ears and nose.

Word of these accidents travels fast, if not always accurately, around a small fishing community. When we got into Newlyn there was a crowd on the pier, all wondering if it was their family's turn for bad news. I saw Wugg's mother, who happened to live alongside me at the time, and I called her to come down to the boat. Looking anxious, but obviously not prepared for anything worse than injury, she came aboard. 'Where is he?' I told her he was aft and before I could say anything else she butted in, 'I'll go down and cheer him up then.'

A chill went through me. I asked her to go up into my cabin for a minute. I knew there was nothing for it but to tell her the facts straight. 'Look I'm sorry, Pam, but Wugg's dead.' As I started to tell her what had happened she just leapt into the corner of my bunk, rolled herself into a tight ball and wept. She sobbed so violently that I had to fetch the doctor to come up and help her.

An uneasy silence fell over the crowd as we took Wugg ashore wrapped in a sheet, except for his head which we left uncovered as a mark of last respect. I could imagine all on the pier feeling guilty at the relief that this time at least it wasn't them grieving.

The most traumatic part of the whole sad event for me was when I was asked to go to the mortuary to identify his body. I can smell that terrible earthy aroma in the room, like a sort of all-pervading damp. The policeman was there, along with the technician who unceremoniously pulled the tray out from the cooler and started pulling Wugg's body about so I should see his face. I was incensed. 'Hey! That's Wuggy Coxon there!' which at least stopped him pulling the poor chap about. Not long after it happened I was talking to Edwin the lifeboat coxswain about how badly I'd taken the mortuary. He told me that he had the same feelings when he'd been with people who moved bodies about as though they were sacks of potatoes. I suppose it's just a job to the technicians and they don't think what effect this seemingly careless attitude can have on others.

There was an inquiry into the incident, an anxious time because we had to wait months for the result. Wugg's father was a naval man and wanted to see things done properly. He brought a solicitor down from London in an attempt to discover if I'd been negligent in any way. A sample of the chain was taken away and the breaking strain measured at thirty-eight tons. The local policeman, who had been a fisherman, made a model of the boat, with all the derricks and gear, which was used to explain the workings of a trawler.

Even though I knew there hadn't been any fault on my part, a cloud hung over me every day until the verdict of accidental death was announced.

Strange as it may seem, you have to accept that disasters are all part of our way of life and, tragic as these events are, they never seem to touch you as closely as a close friend's death in far less tragic or dramatic circumstances. We knew we'd done everything we could to keep Wugg alive even though it was to no avail. You just have to accept the risks as part of the job and get on with it.

The biggest surprise after the accident was when Wuggy's brother came down the pier and asked if he could come to sea with me. When we were at sea we talked about the accident a few times, but it wasn't until we got chatting one evening up in the wheelhouse that suddenly a vivid image returned, one which had disappeared from my mind completely. Wuggy had been the cook on board and had the unusual habit of making out a menu every night, hardly the norm aboard trawlers. I can remember him coming up to the wheelhouse that night and saying, 'We're going to have Toad in the Hole tonight.' The image of him standing next to me at the chart table writing out his menu is the last I have of him alive. I've never had Toad in the Hole since then.

8 JUNE I LEFT HOME for this trip under a bit of a cloud. Nell was none too pleased that I'd spent the second of my two days ashore off drinking with a few of the lads. We didn't speak from when I came home from the pub to the time I came on board yesterday. I wasn't alone in being glad to get back to sea. As we passed Mousehole Island Jiggy came up into the wheelhouse to blow the hooter to his family, and Graham looked across at the village in thoughtful mood. You can just see his house next to the Ship Inn as you steam by and I asked him why he wasn't going to signal to Jan. 'I don't think that would be a very welcome gesture today,' he grinned ruefully. 'Had a bit of a set-to over the weekend. I tried buying flowers but that only made it worse.' He explained that he too had spent most of the day in his pub, watching football, and had rolled in late and with the benefit of a few drinks. Hopefully everything will be forgotten in both our households by the time we get back in.

I have to say that relationships are not a fisherman's strongest point. It takes a pretty independent woman to tolerate the life both are forced to lead; it's hard at sea, but just as hard for the one left at home. The women have a lot to put up with which I'm sure we don't always appreciate or even think about.

They have to cope with bringing up a family practically singlehanded, with the constant worry about the danger their partner faces through bad weather and mechanical failure. In addition to creating problems at sea, either can bring financial hardship as well. Since we only get paid when we catch fish there's the temptation to risk carrying on fishing when it would be more sensible to stop.

The women have to put aside money when they can for the times when there's no income, which can be for periods of weeks, even months. Mortgages and bills still need to be paid, and the family still have to eat. They have to become hardened to it all, learn to make all the decisions and cope with any crisis life throws at them. I'm sure the worry of hearing about bad weather and imminent gale force winds is worse for them than it is for us out here. At least these days we have the phone to keep in touch, when we're in range. The kids can tell dad what's been going on at school and dad can tell them that the weather's not as bad as it sounds on the forecast.

81

It's all the little occurrences in life – the things that build up a basis for family life – that you miss out on when you spend most of your life away. The phrase 'You never told me that' must have cropped up thousands of times, when all those seemingly unimportant bits of news were forgotten by the time you got in. The phone does have its disadvantages, mind you. The women can check up what day, even the time, the boat's going to be back in port. In the past it was quite easy to sneak back into harbour and have a good old time before arriving home. It used to be nothing for Nellie to hear the door open unexpectedly and find me stumbling in the worse for wear, and get up to cook me a meal in the early hours.

It breaks my heart when Nellie tells me that Sophie's been asking, 'Will Dad be home for my birthday?' and she has to say, 'We'll have to see.' You never want to say that you definitely will be in because you never know, and there's nothing worse for children than a series of broken promises. It's the same with everything, weddings, births, christenings – about the only ceremony you're sure of attending is your own funeral. I sometimes wonder how many first teeth, first steps, first days at school, or wins at sports days are missed across the country by fishermen. I was at sea for 280 days last year, which means that chances are you are away for most things. Mind you there are some things I don't mind missing, first nappy change, potty training, and teething. A conventional family life for a fisherman is pie in the sky, the women really have to face bringing up families as single parents.

We can be difficult to live with when we are on shore. Fishermen tend to be big spenders, generous when the money is there, with not much thought for the times when it will inevitably disappear. It's difficult for the women to understand how we can spend so much money between landing and walking through the door. It starts when the wages are settled up in the pub, a time to relax and unwind, catch up on the news from the other boys who've been to sea. Stories, prices, fishing grounds, and a few drinks are all exchanged before there's any thought of going home. Then it's home by taxi with the wages already not burning quite such a large hole in your pocket. Through the front door. If the children are there it's: 'Dad's home!' so back into town on a shopping spree. There's only two days before going back to sea for another ten, so make the most of it. The kids love it but Mum is left wondering if there'll be enough money left over to stretch until the next landing day.

These homecomings can be traumatic: fraught in the mildest cases, dreaded in some households. Dad arrives through the door much the worse for wear, with a small bag of fish, a large bag of washing and a wage packet which is already smaller than it was hours before. The bags have hardly been cleared away and he's in the chair snoring away, and the dinner's ruined. It would be very easy to spend the next two days arguing, but you know you've only got forty-eight hours so it's forgive and forget and get on with it. Then back to sea.

If I'm honest there's many a time when this return to sea is an escape from all the trappings of family life. I dread to think how many men go back down that pier leaving arguments unsettled, problems unsolved, hoping they will be forgotten before the next landing.

Christmas can be one of the worst times of stress for both partners. She's not used to having him around, tending to view him as a bit of an intrusion. After the first couple of days he's bored to tears by the prospect of being stuck ashore for two weeks. By the end of the fortnight everyone is just about getting used to each other, or at least tolerating one another, when it's time to head back down the pier again.

January's a bad time financially as well, which adds to the tensions. Everyone's overspent at Christmas, there's been no money for two weeks, no prospect of any for another ten days, and then only if the weather's good enough for a fair catch. I'm sure there are not many happy New Years in fishermen's families.

Landlocked friends find it difficult to understand why you can't plan ahead. There must be thousands of invitations which have to be given the reply 'We'll have to see.' After a few attempts you're often struck off the list the next time. Then when your partner does plan something for herself you turn up unannounced and everything has to change because the last thing you need is a house full of people when you just want to slump in the chair. All arrangements are made with an 'if' or 'perhaps' attached. Those friends who don't understand fall by the wayside very quickly. Nellie's quite used to going out to dinner with friends on her own because I've still been at sea or, if I do go along, to me falling asleep in the soup.

When two-thirds of your life is spent at sea you have to learn to live two separate lives. There has to be a lot more give and take on both sides than in most relationships. The marriages which do survive the early years usually last and become rock solid. On our boat Tony has been married to Gwyneth for thirty-five years, and Bobby has been married to Inez for thirty-eight. Each half has to learn to stick to their own role, and be happy with it. My first partner was a lady who could cope with it all.

When I was young most girls wanted to get married as quickly as possible so they could do exactly the same thing as their mothers had been doing for the last thirty years: scrubbing and scrimping to keep family and home together against all odds. They'd seen their fathers working their arses off to keep the kids and when they'd got the chance they just wanted to jump on the same relentless treadmill as their mums. I knew I couldn't be doing with getting involved with someone who wanted that, so I kept myself pretty free and I have to confess I went a bit mad with the maids in my mid-teens. My first long-term relationship came about by accident, not design.

I was over in Mousehole at a party one evening when the deep-throated roar of an old Jaguar told us that Joan had arrived. We smiled hello as she passed and I spent a raucous evening in another room talking to some of the other fishermen. I'd been at school with her son, Brennan, and Joan's dad and mine were great drinking partners so I'd seen her about the place. She looked as though she had gypsy blood, with her striking long black hair, and haunting deep brown eyes. She was an intelligent, cultured lady who could talk with confidence about the latest style of painting and who knew exactly which knife and fork to use when. I was sixteen and living in a little cellar down under the newsagents overlooking Mousehole harbour, a sanctuary where, in between fishing trips, I'd spend hours painting.

I left the party with the last few serious drinkers and was walking back along the harbour side when I came across Joan's car. I could smell the leather of the seats as I leant down to wish her goodnight. She smiled and explained that she couldn't start the engine. I shrugged, 'Well, don't worry, come home to my place.'

I never thought much about it, my home was only about twenty yards away. We went down into the small room with its double bed, surrounded by paintings. I can see her now in her canvas duckfrock, a sort of smock with a rounded neck and two pockets, and her two red spotted scarves, one knotted around her head the other used as her handbag containing all she needed: car keys, lipstick and purse. We closed the door, put the kettle on, and that was that.

84

Next morning she phoned her brother who came over and got her car going. 'OK I'll see you,' was all she said as a parting comment. I didn't think much about it and spent most of the day in the Swordfish pub having a few beers. Later in the evening she came in, had a drink and I went home with her where I stayed for the next thirteen happy years.

I reckon it was about the best thing I could ever have done at that time of my life, getting together with Joan, a beautiful olive-skinned, sophisticated, bright thirty-eight-year-old. It must have been a strange combination to outsiders. She was gentle and arty, I was a fisherman; almost diametrically opposed characters.

My mum used to ask, 'You living with that woman?' I would reply yes, and she'd say, 'You be careful now!' Knowing very well what she was getting at I'd ask, 'What d'you mean?' She'd give me an old-fashioned look, 'Well you know what it's like what you get up to,' and I'd say 'Yeh, I know what we get up to.'

My Old Man used to sit there puffing away at his pipe pretending not to listen to the ritual exchange, but as she left the room he'd look up at me and wink. He loved it all.

Joan was a working artist, creating all sorts of things. She was also a model and sat for painters like Harold Harvey and Dod Proctor, whose portrait of her, 'The Smiling Girl', used to hang in the Royal Academy. Nell's daughter Shevie, who is now studying at art college, couldn't believe that I knew people like Dod Proctor, but they were in and out all the time, and I never took much notice of them.

We lived a wonderfully free life. I'd go to sea in the winter, then spend the summer ashore playing around in Joan's pottery before going back to sea for another season.

This was in the early Sixties and we used to supply the small touristy craft shops with pottery bits and pieces. I'd do my bit by carving fish on them. We'd drive off in her old car with a basket full of pottery, sell it to the shops and end up going home with thirty or forty quid in our pockets. We could live on this for a long time until there wasn't much more than a few coppers left and Joan would say, 'Time for another firing'. Then we'd set to work making another load.

Artists had always been part of our lives in Newlyn from as early as I could remember. The old quay was a very good place to paint, with all the old pilchard nets hanging down over the colourful buoys and crab pots, and the small boats painted in their bright colours pulled up along the beach all higgledy-piggledy.

With the old boys working away at the nets it was such a scene of possibilities.

I often look back to some of the painters I used to see around the harbour and think how similar their lives were to fishermen in the way they lived from hand to mouth. There was one old boy I remember who was regularly down the quay knocking off pictures of the harbour that were quite brilliant. While the oil was still wet he'd go off and sell his latest masterpiece for a few quid in order to have enough money to go back and buy a few drinks. That was how we all used to live, fishermen and painters alike.

The artistic community in the Sixties was centred around St Ives and was flourishing. It was close knit and looked upon with suspicion by most of the locals, probably with some reason considering the wild parties which were a regular part of the scene. It was nothing unusual to turn round and end up spilling red wine all over someone like Barbara Hepworth; they were all just around and about.

It was simple, easy living, maybe because I was younger and didn't have to worry about the ins and outs of paying bills, or dragging myself out of bed early in the morning to start work. We never had an awful lot of material possessions to worry about. When I was at sea, I'd come home with a basket of fish, give a few to the old boys in the village, swop some for some eggs or bread and we'd eat the rest ourselves. When I was ashore for whatever reason I would go out with my lurcher catching rabbits and at least we could eat well. It was all a lot easier. We cooked on a primus stove in the summer because the old Cornish range would have made the place too hot, and when we wanted a roast dinner we'd fire up the pottery kiln.

Our favourite pub was The Gurnard's Head hotel over at Zennor, run by Jimmy and Daphne Goodman. We used to go up there and say to Jimmy, 'We've got no money at the moment,' and he'd let us just drink away all night. The next time I came in from sea I'd take him up a few bags of fish. The Goodmans had something of a cult following in the area; people would go there just to watch them having rows. They never installed a cash register in the bar; they just rolled up bundles of notes and stuffed them into cracks around the old Aga in the kitchen round the back.

I was up there drinking on my own once at about four or five in the morning having consumed a fair quantity of alcohol when Daphne said to me, 'Just as well you go up and sleep in Jimmy's bed.' Jimmy was a great cricketer and often used to take himself off to Lord's to watch a match, as he had done on this occasion. When he arrived home at about seven o'clock the following morning he discovered me in his bed, 'What the bloody hell are you doing there?' he roared, carefully emphasizing every word, as though each was its own sentence, to add weight to his question. It was a fair point, but the problem was I couldn't think why I was there. I wasn't really sure how he was going to react, but it wasn't that much of an unusual occurrence so he just wandered off without saying anything more. More important to him, his team had won so we went downstairs to share a bottle of champagne.

It was like that all the time. You'd be up there in the winter with the winds howling around the building, then suddenly the lights would go. Flicker, flicker, darkness. There would be a lot of fumbling around under the bar before the old oil lights came out, and for a while there'd be a great atmosphere. Then you'd see Jimmy stumble outside and with a lot of muttering and cursing he'd start up the old generator. Then the light bulbs would reluctantly flicker back into life.

'Nothing flash, Goodman's the name,' was his barked greeting which was a lie, because he'd been a captain in the 1st Airborne Division during the war and won several different bravery awards. But to strangers he must have appeared a miserable old cuss.

Although there was never any question of keeping legal opening hours, it was always a matter of luck whether or not customers were served at any time of the day. Visitors used to come in at lunchtime just after two o'clock when the place was full of locals ordering drinks. As they walked over to the bar, they'd smile at him but before they could even say hello, Jimmy would growl, 'We're closed. Shut the door when you leave.' It was really quite embarrassing at times. There was an army house down in the cliffs where soldiers would train to abseil, and quite often they would come in and ask for twenty halves of shandy. Jimmy would reply, 'Haven't got any,' and turn his back. No matter how much they tried he'd never serve them because he couldn't be bothered with all that effort for such little return. I'm surprised it never came to blows.

Everyone used to go there from the local arty gang, and with the fishermen and farmers as well it was a great mixture. Could they drink in quantity and at length! We used to have a party nearly every Saturday night at the Gurnard's Head. It was a great time. Most of the characters have gone now, never to be replaced, and my world is all the duller for their absence.

87

In her fifty-second year Joan complained of feeling unwell. Cancer was diagnosed. She said she didn't want me to be near her, but wrote a letter explaining her feelings for me and how it would be best to remember her as she'd been: the smiling girl of Dod Proctor's painting.

Three weeks later, back at sea, I woke up for no apparent reason, turned out of my bunk and sat on the chart table with my sleeping bag wrapped around me to guard against the cold of the unheated cabin. I had the big radio set on and it wasn't long before I heard Joan's daughter, Bella, calling the ship. I knew what had happened. I was prepared for it because I knew she was dying, it was the funeral I couldn't stand. It was touch and go whether I went or not, but in the end I did.

There are times even now when I'm sat out here in the wheelhouse I think to myself that maybe she's looking down at me.

My twenty-ninth year turned out to be a traumatic one. A few months before Joan was taken ill I'd been up to Brixham to pick up a beamer to bring it back to Newlyn. Joan phoned me there to tell me that my sister was very ill in hospital and I should get back as soon as possible. She had a congenital heart problem, which had suddenly become worse. There was a chap with me who drove a Ford Capri who offered to take me back. I knew that he would use the excuse to put his foot down, and I can't stand fast driving so I waited for Joan to drive up to collect me. When I arrived at the hospital my sister had died. If I'd taken the lift I would have been there in time. I've never forgiven myself. I returned to fetch the beamer back to Newlyn a couple of weeks after her funeral. It was on that trip that the youngster Wuggy was killed. Not long after that my late sister's husband committed suicide by shooting himself. Then a couple of months later Joan died, and so it went on. Within the space of two years I lost my father, lover, sister, uncle, aunt and a crew member. I had been prepared for my dad's departure because he'd had a hard life and he knew he was dying, but the rest were terrible shocks. It's amazing how the body and brain can cope with it though.

A couple of years later along came Jenny, followed swiftly by my first daughter Demelza and so we got married. She didn't force me into it but I was badgered by my mum and her dad and auntie. They kept on, 'What about Demelza? You ought to marry the girl for her sake.' In the end just to keep the peace I said that I would.

I got dressed up in a suit, wore a tie and even combed my hair, three firsts in my life. Jenny breezed into the registrar's office in an old dress with flip flops flapping at her heels looking like a bag of rags and smiled, 'Come on, let's get on with it.' But she was so vivacious you could forgive her anything.

It was not a match made in heaven, however. As my old mum used to mutter, 'As God made them, he paired them.' A few years later we went our separate ways.

Relationships in our community must look odd to outsiders but when you get fed up with somebody, or nine times out of ten they get fed up with you, you move on. Often you find that people have ended up swopping partners and I'm sure if you went away for a period of time and came back it could be very confusing. It's all pretty inevitable when men are away for so long so often, and it's not peculiar to fishing either.

After Jenny I had several girlfriends before Nell came along. She'd been married to Terry, one of the arty gang we used to mix with, and we'd often go off to parties as a group. At around the same time that I parted company with Jenny, Terry had also gone his own way from Nellie. We happened to meet up one evening in the Coastguard hotel and that was that really. Nell and Terry's daughter Shevie was about three at the time and we ended up living a few hundred yards away from Terry and his new partner, Sally. In fact we all got along well, so well that we used to spend a fair amount of time together.

Nellie and I have weathered many storms for fifteen years now. In 1985 Sophie was born. She brought a new dimension to our lives and the prospect of going to sea week in, week out has seemed less attractive ever since.

———————————

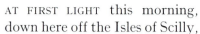 AT FIRST LIGHT this morning, down here off the Isles of Scilly, we were passed by a couple of racing yachts setting off across the Atlantic on this year's single-handed transatlantic race. I told Mitch, who was on watch, to give them plenty of sea-room. I've had all the dealings I want to with these large, very expensive yachts sailed by tough competitive people, and I get a bit twitchy if we get too close to them.

Eight years ago to the week we were fishing in this same area and I was down in the galley having a bite to eat when there was a call from the wheelhouse.

'Roger, there's a bit of a distress on up here.' I rushed up in time to hear Falmouth coastguard calling for assistance from any vessels in our area. The weather was so bad that we were one of the few boats around so I called up offering our help, even though we were about an hour away from the position they'd given. They explained that a racing trimaran called *Bachelor Sweet Pea* had turned turtle while taking part in the single-handed race from Plymouth to New York. Her English skipper, June Clark, was sitting on the upturned hull waiting for help. The *Esso Tenby*, an oil tanker, was already on the scene but was really too big to be able to do much.

We brought our gear aboard and set off. As we steamed along we heard that the Penlee lifeboat, the *Mabel Alice*, had been launched and was also on its way. As we got nearer we heard the coxswain ask the tanker to send a flare up so that they could get a fix. By the time we arrived the lifeboat had already taken the sailor off the yacht and although the woman wasn't hurt they dashed her back to Penzance so she could be checked over in hospital. We were asked to take the trimaran in tow back to Newlyn and the *Esso Tenby* went on her way.

It was quite a job because the trimaran still had the sails set under the water which made her drag, but we plodded our way back. We were forced to stop just outside the harbour when the top of the yacht's mast hit the seabed, not surprising since it must have been sticking down nearly fifty feet under the water. We got a diver out to cut away the steel rigging to release the mast so the hull could be taken alongside the quay where a crane lifted it out.

Up on dry land we had a good look at the boat. June Clark must have been tough. To escape from the upturned hull she'd had to crawl into one of the floats and unscrew masses of screws holding the escape panel in place, underwater all the time. We didn't think much more about the whole incident; no one had been hurt and although it wasn't the reason we'd offered help, we felt that at least we'd get a few bob for a decent salvage tow. We had a couple of beers and went home, ready to set off to sea again twenty-four hours later.

The next morning there were some reporters sniffing around the harbour, talking to people about the rescue. Before long one came over and asked me what I had to say about the allegations that I'd tried to push the yachtswoman off the capsized boat so that I could claim salvage. I couldn't believe it, I just didn't know what to say. Apart from the fact that I just wouldn't do that sort of thing, I knew that she was well away from the yacht by the time we got there.

I stormed off across the harbour to the lifeboat building with a string of reporters running behind me to ask Kenny, the coxswain, to tell the story as he'd witnessed it. Unfortunately Kenny had already gone back to sea so I couldn't get him to back me up. The only person there was the engineer. 'Come out here a minute and tell these reporters what happened,' I asked him. I didn't really understand his response.

'If I come out will you hit me?'

I said, 'If you don't come out I'll kill you!' A figure of speech of course. For some reason best known to himself he didn't come out to put the story straight, but the reporters heard all of this exchange. I knew there wasn't much more I could do so I just shrugged my shoulders, left it at that and went back to sea.

A couple of days later, on the Sunday, another Newlyn skipper who'd just left harbour steamed to find us with that morning's papers. We came alongside and he threw them aboard. We were stunned. The story of the rescue was nothing like we remembered it. There were all sorts of allegations about me pushing June Clark off her yacht and one that I'd threatened to kill the lifeboat's engineer when he wouldn't corroborate my side of the story. In one paper I was referred to as a pirate, in another I was a cowboy, and Newlyn was supposed to be full of rusty old boats. Billy Stevenson, who'd done his good deed by letting one of his trawlers carry out the tow, was described in terms which didn't make him very happy. I can't remember the exact words but it was something like a little short man with a tam and rusty boats, which was when the fun really started.

I was prepared to give June Clark the benefit of the doubt, perhaps she had been dazed and confused, but Billy was straight on the phone to the lawyers. We'd done all we could to help this person and suddenly we were the villains of the hour.

When I returned to port I went over to the trimaran where June Clark was removing anything she could unscrew, and had a chat with her about what was going on. She was adamant that I'd virtually rammed her yacht while she was still on it just to push her off. I didn't say much, since I knew she'd already gone by the time we arrived to tow the boat, but just listened, trying to work out what was really in her mind. One of the things she said had happened was that she'd shouted up at the line of crew standing on my deck and that I had a foreigner aboard who'd shouted back. Obviously I knew we hadn't got anyone more foreign than a Penzance man aboard us, but it suddenly dawned on me what might be the confusion in her mind. The conversation had probably been with the tanker's crew. I kept quiet about my thoughts in case we needed to take the whole thing any further in court later on.

The papers were told exactly what had happened and they printed an apology, but it was so small that we still took them to court where the captain of the Esso tanker clinched the matter. He sent in a report which told the whole story of how the sailor had already been put aboard the lifeboat before we turned up, and we were in the clear. We won damages from the papers, made a few quid from the salvage claim but in the end it was a whole load of hassle that wasn't worth it.

A couple of days later Mitch, who was then on another boat, towed up June Clark's wallet, full of dollar and sterling notes, credit cards and so on. Do you know he never even got a thank you from her.

This year's yachts are being left well alone.

  YOU'D THINK WORLD WAR III had broken out in Newlyn today. It was the main story on the television news; questions were asked in parliament; journalists swarmed all over the place – a complete overreaction to a little ongoing row with the French.

We were down off the Scillies when we had a visit from HMS *Brecon*, another of Her Majesty's fishery protection vessels. I think I've made my feelings about being boarded quite clear so I won't add much except to say that everything was legal and she went on her way quite happily. Then Graham came back to the galley saying that all hell was let loose on the radio, with some boats asking HMS *Brecon* for assistance.

Three small Newlyn boats fishing with gill nets had come to blows with a couple of large French trawlers, which was how this international incident had started. The trawlers had towed down right through the nets of the Newlyn boys, destroying thousands of pounds' worth of gear, and apparently treating it all as a good lark. It's nothing new; as long as I can remember there have been conflicts between boats using different fishing methods, often between boats from the same port as well. At a time when there's less fish around, the hunt for those remaining few is bound to become intensely competitive.

Although there are hundreds of variations, there are four main different types of fishing in this country: lines, trawls, purse seines and tangle nets. The simplest method has always been to throw out several miles of line with hooks every few yards. It's still favoured by the Spaniards hunting for hake, because they like the quality of the fish they catch, and they still have plenty of cheap labour to work the lines.

Lining had its satisfying moments especially when you were pulling the line in and you could feel the fish on the hooks. The old skate would puff themselves out against your pull, give in for a while as they became tired, then you'd feel a sudden pull as they resisted again. It was a great sight when there were fish floating on the surface, caught on the hooks, as far as you could see and you just couldn't gut them as fast as they were brought aboard. I've been on lining boats when there've been so many fish that you were up to your thighs in them, and all you could do would be to stand there taking them off the hooks as they came aboard.

The *William Sampson* is a beam trawler towing a pair of eight-metre long steel beams across the seabed. Behind each beam comes several tons of chain mat which digs into the sand and kicks bottom-feeding fish up into the open mouth of the net, which is also attached to the beams. The fish are then funnelled along the huge cone of the net into the cod end. In theory smaller fish escape through the mesh along the way, leaving the correct sized ones to

ABOVE Lowering the beam and chain   RIGHT Mending the nets

be brought on board after every four hours towing around. It's pretty brutal, and not particularly skilful: we simply scoop up everything in our path, including boulders, tin cans and any other rubbish on the seabed. The only things which will really cause us problems are large wrecks; anything else just gets smashed up by the weight of the beam and the chain. In the North Sea some of the bigger beamers are towing up to 32 tons of gear which is terrible really. It must do untold damage to the seabed, flattening out the areas of rocky ground which should be havens for fish to breed in.

I've noticed the number of ray purses being washed up on the beaches have increased, and I'm convinced this is all connected with the way that beamers are scatting hell out of the seabed. When the ray lays her eggs they are in a purse-like cocoon which fastens itself to a rock by a little spiral tentacle. This fastening is so strong that no matter how strong the tide is, it won't get pulled off. The skin of the cocoon is too tough for any fish to eat so the eggs will survive safely. That is until a damn great beam trawler comes along towing tons of gear through the seabed.

I don't care who knows I've said this but we're just destroying the sea. It simply will not stand it. I've been out there for thirty-two years now and I've seen it getting worse and worse. With all the electronic navigational aids we now have we know our position to within a hundred feet, so we can tow right up to and around any obstacle that's marked on our charts. In the past when we couldn't be so accurate we were forced to give wrecks a wider berth so much more ground would be left alone, often the best breeding grounds as well. Now we leave very few stones unturned.

The side and stern trawlers, like the Frenchmen involved in the confrontation off the Isles of Scilly today, work the seabed with one net and without a beam or any of this chain. They just skim the seabed. The net's kept open by two otter boards attached to either side of the mouth. These boards are set at such an angle that as they are towed along, the force of the water pushes them away from each other, keeping the mouth of the net open. Without the protection of beam and chain they have to be careful not to snag the net on rocks or wrecks which would rip it apart.

Both types of trawling catch the same types of bottom-feeding fish, but side and stern trawlers don't pick up too much muck and rubbish from the seabed, and their fish tends to come out of the net in a better condition because it's not been pummelled around by being dragged over rough ground.

You can see cycles in the fashions for these types of fishing.

Beam trawling is nothing new: traditional sailing trawlers were using wooden beams at the end of the last century. Up in Grimsby a steam tug was used to tow the sailing trawlers out to sea where they could pick up the wind. One day when there was no wind, they decided to tow the sailing trawler with its beam down. Then someone had the bright idea of using the tug itself to tow a trawl and the first power driven trawler was created.

They decided they could use bigger nets without a beam by using otter boards to keep the net open. Things went full circle when the large trawlers with huge engines came along and they could return to beams, but this time much heavier steel versions which the new power could tow at high speed.

There's another type of trawling using seine nets. The conical net has two long lines, one attached to either side of the open mouth. Each warp is made up of around 1500 fathoms of rope, nearly two miles. The end of one warp is attached to an anchor which is dropped overboard; then the boat steams off in a huge semicircle, paying out the line as it goes. When they reach the end of this first line the net is dropped overboard and the boat completes a circle back to the buoy with the other warp. Back at the anchor, the boat sits in the water and pulls in the two warps using a powerful winch. These lengthy ropes thrash the seabed as they're pulled in, disturbing fish over the large area between them and shepherding the catch into the net as the circle closes. When more powerful boats came along they towed at the same time as they hauled and so covered an even greater area of the seabed.

The third and most modern method of fishing is purse seining. They use great twenty ton nets, nearly three hundred fathoms long and seventy fathoms deep, to catch the type of fish known as pelagic which swim near the surface, like mackerel, herring and pilchards. They find a patch of fish and shoot the net around the shoal in a big circle. The top of the net is held on the surface by floats while the bottom sinks down creating a cylindrical wall around the shoal. Then the bottom is drawn together trapping the fish in what effectively has then become a huge purse. The whole net is drawn together, concentrating the fish into a small corral, until a pipe can be put over the side to suck the fish into the ship's hold. In this country the Scots are the main users of this method.

The Newlyn boys who had the trouble with the Frenchmen today were working at the other end of the scale, on the fourth type of fishing, tangle netting, which traps fish by their gills in either fixed or drifting nets. Fixed nets are anchored to the seabed, usually around a wreck. Plastic floats attached to the top of the net and weights at the bottom keep the net like a wall. Then the boats just wait for the fish to get caught by their gills in the fine mesh. These netters have to fish at slack water because strong tides roll the nets over each other and they become a mess. It's not so good for the lads today because we reckon the tides are higher and therefore running more fiercely than the tide tables show. You only have to look at the old high waterline in Newlyn to see that it was well below the level of today's high tides, which must be part of the whole changing weather scene. There's no way that thirty years ago we had storms like we do today and you only have to look around at some of the really old quays to see that they wouldn't protect you much from today's weather, yet they must have been fine when they were built.

The other type of tangle netting is drifting. The boat shoots a long net overboard near a pilchard or mackerel shoal, usually hanging down at about two fathoms, and the boat drifts along with the nets which can be miles long.

So you have all these different methods competing for fish in the same areas. From what we could hear on the radio today these two particular French trawlers became annoyed that the nets were set in the areas they wanted to trawl so instead of moving to another piece of ground, or towing around them, they simply towed right through them. Despite all the fuss, it really is nothing new. There's always been a tension between these particular methods of fishing because the netters effectively block off a whole area of the sea to the trawlers. There are no rules about who has priority – it's always been worked on a friendly basis. But there are far more netters in Newlyn now. From half a dozen when I was a boy, I should say there are nigh on sixty of them now, so we've got to work out a better system of cooperation. When I was on netters or even long liners, we would steam up to the trawlers and throw across the positions of our gear, written on a piece of paper tied around something like a can of beans. There have been some examples of netters setting their gear then steaming off leaving them, so there's been no way of knowing where the nets lie until you find them on the end of your beam when you haul. Some of them have been leaving five or six thousand pounds' worth of nets out there while they've gone back into port and expected them to survive. So it's not always the trawler's fault.

It will be interesting to get back into Newlyn to find out what happened in today's incident.

PREVIOUS PAGES Newlyn harbour
ABOVE AND RIGHT At work on the chain mats

ABOVE Graham and Tony watching the nets come in
RIGHT Emptying the nets

LEFT Clearing the nets   TOP Sorting the catch
ABOVE Washing the rubbish over the side

ABOVE The catch on deck   LEFT Steaming home
PAGES 110–11 Gutting the fish

PREVIOUS PAGES, LEFT AND ABOVE Unloading
the catch from the hold in harbour
OVERLEAF AND PAGE 118 Newlyn fish market

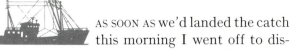
AS SOON AS we'd landed the catch this morning I went off to discover what the real story had been with World War III. Over at the net store on the old quay I bumped into Nicky Cripps, a netter skipper. He told me that these two French trawlers were well known for causing trouble. He'd had all his turbot gear, 100,000 yards of net, worth twenty to thirty thousand pounds, towed away probably by these same two boats over the years. He said that most of the French trawlers were cooperative, but these two from Concarneau had always gone out of their way to be difficult. They are both company boats and the general feeling is that the skippers couldn't care less about what they do because they don't own their boats and aren't worried about damaging their gear but only about catching as many fish in as short a time as possible. Even their fellow countrymen have had trouble with them.

I was on my way back over to share the catch money with the boys when I saw a lad from one of the netters involved in the argument coming up the quay. The story is quite unbelievable really. He told me how they'd given the Frenchman the readings of where their gear was lying and he'd ignored this completely, towing right through the whole lot. That's more than bad luck, it's precision sabotage. Then I met Mervyn, another of the victims, who said the worst thing he could have done was to give him the exact readings, because it made it easier for the Frenchman to cause the maximum damage out of spite. We'd seen pictures on the television news of the navy removing one of the netter's anchors from the French trawler which the crew must have been keeping as a trophy. Mervyn told me that all the French crew were out on the deck laughing at them, even playing the Marseillaise over their tannoy system. It must have been something of an old feud between the boats, because this time someone on the French boat threw bits of old iron chain and bars down at the netter. Mervyn said they involved the navy this time because it was the only way they could stop the whole lot being towed away. As it was they lost about a third of all the nets.

All this rivalry between fishermen from different places and using different methods goes back years. We even had trouble in Newlyn at the end of the last century when east coast fishermen came down to fish our waters on a Sunday when they knew the locals would be observing the Sabbath. It was too much for our ancestors, and the Newlyn men laid into the blackguards. Soldiers were drafted in from Plymouth to restore order.

We had trouble a few years back with the big Russian factory ships. Eastern bloc nations have always been great eaters of pelagic fish, so they have these huge ships which go off for months at a time to catch, process and tin the fish. There were angry scenes down here when they descended on the south-west and caught so much of our fish that they were in danger of wiping out our stocks. I remember the sight of our small wooden fishing boats alongside these huge factory ships, just off Land's End, with fists being waved. The Russians became part of the scene for a while and we'd often trawl up tins from the boats, which perhaps had been thrown overboard because they weren't up to scratch.

Sheltering from bad weather years ago we steamed into St Ives bay where we found about thirty Polish, Russian and Romanian factory trawlers. When the weather improved I said to the lads that we should send across some entertainment, so we gathered up the few girlie magazines we had on board, tied them up with string, steamed across to one of the Poles and threw the package aboard. The men, who were working away in their fur hats with flaps over their ears, watched all this but not one moved to pick the magazines up. We could see why. There was a foreman stood on the afterdeck who just shook his head. This was at the height of the cold war and I suppose there was a deep mistrust of all things western, though I reckon they went straight up the wheelhouse for the skipper.

Some of these ships had more aerials and bits and pieces up their masts than we'd ever seen on any fishing boats. It was strange because they used to come into Mount's Bay with all this electronic equipment, just a few miles away from the naval air station at Culdrose where the anti-submarine helicopter training took place.

All that changed when we introduced our own 200-mile territorial waters, and we haven't seen them since. Now we've got to contend with our neighbours, who are getting ever nearer. As Jiggy said in the pub as we sorted out the wages, 'We've spent hundreds of years trying to keep the French out. Now we're building a tunnel to let them back in.' I'm sure this weekend's confrontation won't be the last fun.

———————

 THE BBC RADIO announcer read the Midnight Thirty shipping forecast in gentle soothing tones, making it sound like a shopping list. When it came to Sole, Lundy, Fastnet she reassuringly reported our sea conditions as a gentle force three or four. I nearly fell off the wheelhouse chair. If that was the case the *William Sampson* was having me on, doing a very good impersonation of a ship in a storm. As the pleasant female voice told me she was making her way home now and wished me a quiet night I looked at the waves breaking over the boat and imagined her returning to her nice warm, and stationary, house.

I weaved my way below to wake the boys up to haul, down the steps from the wheelhouse into the alleyway then dodging the galley door as it flung itself back against the deckhead. I put the kettle on the hot plate before climbing down the ladder into the sleeping quarters which shudder and shake as the propeller lifts out of the water and searches for something to bite on before being plunged back into the sea with the next wave. Even with the noise of the engine thundering through the bulkhead, the screaming of the screw, and all the other crashes down there below the waterline,

Watching television in the galley

I could hear Mitch's snoring. As I turned on the lights and moved across to wake each man in turn, Jiggy was already halfway out of his bunk – he never really seems to sleep. 'What's going on here then?' he asked sternly in mock anger, and we watched as Mitch emerged slowly and reluctantly. He always looks as though he's just gone five rounds with Frank Bruno when he wakes up, his deep sunken eyes all puffed up with deep grey bags under them.

Tony crawled out of his hole, last as ever, and sat for a few moments on the bench composing himself before leaping into action with the speed of a striking snail. Only Graham was allowed to sleep on, it being his turn for extra kip.

As I held the grabrail with one hand and poured steaming water into my mug, I told Jiggy that the weather forecast was force three, and he threw his head back in one of his hyena laughs as he was flung against the table by another pitch of the boat.

The worst thing for the boys in this sort of weather is the effort required to put on extra clothing when you're half asleep. 'Never mind, soon be back in bed again, boys!' Jiggy cried as he climbed out on to the deck.

No matter how many years I do this job I still sometimes get twitchy up here in the wheelhouse in the middle of the night if my imagination runs too wild. It's not helped by idiots like Graham playing tricks on me as he did tonight. It was just after three, an hour after we'd finished sorting and gutting the haul. I'd assumed

ABOVE Shaving in the galley
LEFT Mitch putting on his oilies

all the lads were turned in, getting a couple of hours kip before bringing the nets up again. I went into my cabin to get some more tobacco, and as I turned round a hand grabbed my leg and Graham let out a bloodcurdling yell from behind the cabin door. He must have waited for ages to carry out this surprise.

He's played this, and similar tricks of appearing at the wheelhouse windows, hundreds of times but it still gets me. Jiggy doesn't react at all if you try it on him. I don't know if that's because he has nerves of steel or just slow reactions.

There are times out here when you have to create a bit of fun to alleviate the pressures and boredom. We once had a young lad on board who was fairly new to the sea and we decided he needed an initiation into the joys of being on watch at the dead of night. Before we left port I enlisted the help of some other skippers.

After a couple of days out he came aft to the galley at the end of his watch, looking thoughtful. As casually as possible, already knowing the answer, I asked him, 'What's all the news then?'

With some disbelief he said that he'd heard two skippers talking on the VHF about a cargo ship on which two gorillas had been running around loose. Apparently the ship had been making its way up the Channel taking the animals to a zoo when these gorillas had broken out of a crate on the deck. He explained that they'd shot one but the other had jumped overboard. We told him not to be stupid, but he became quite indignant and went back to the wheelhouse insisting that he was telling the truth.

A few hours later he returned with another snippet about the story which was unfolding over the radio. 'The skipper of the *Altje Adriantje* says a gorilla can swim for days, so it will probably survive.' We told him not to tell such stories and sent him back.

Over the next few days new information about the gorilla trickled in over the radio. He'd been seen making for the Isles of Scilly because he could smell that they were semi-tropical. Then it was revealed that it was a silverback. 'Aren't they the really big ones?' our lad asked with concern. I told him that I didn't know anything about them; all I knew was that there was obviously one swimming around out there. Then he would hear a new development and tell us they were flying zoologists to the Scillies to look for him. We were about fifteen miles off the islands at this point.

The skipper's bunk in the wheelhouse

This lad knew everything about the movements of this creature because even when he wasn't on watch he'd come up to the wheelhouse and listen in to the radio conversations between boats. The last overheard discussion was about how easy it would be for a gorilla to grab hold of the trawl cable while a boat was fishing and pull himself up, climb along the derrick and jump down on the deck. The skippers reckoned he'd be an impressive sight reaching up to the height of the wheelhouse windows.

By now the boy could almost see the gorilla in the sea and kept looking around in case it climbed aboard. On watch he was more worried about bumping into that beast than other ships.

This was all happening just after the film *The Planet of the Apes* had been released, and they were selling very authentic looking masks in a shop in town. The lad was left on watch in the early hours after we'd hauled and all hands were making their way back to bed. I took the ape mask I'd bought out of its hiding place, pulled on my black boiler suit and enlisted the engineer's help to spray oil all over me. I must say that I looked awesome.

I waited until the boy was settled into his watch. It was a black night and by now about three o'clock in the morning. I crept along the deck, and climbed up so that my head would appear right outside the wheelhouse window when I stood up. I waited until I could see from his reflection that he'd turned away, then stood up slowly and looked in. He stayed with his back to me and didn't look as though he was going to move so I made a low grunting rattle in my throat. He turned around, stood frozen for a second, then screamed. There before him was that very same dangerous silverback he'd been hearing about for several days. He was so frightened that he lost control of his bodily functions before running aft to the galley screaming, 'Gorilla, gorilla!'

He frightened me just as much as I scared him. I jumped down, tearing the mask and suit off as I went, and fell into the galley just as he was starting to tell the others what he'd seen. He was ashen and sat in the corner curled up and shaking, refusing to move but looking at the door with utter fear in his eyes. That gorilla was on the boat and he wasn't going to take his eyes off the door through which he just *knew* it was going to burst at any moment.

The plan had worked too well; we hadn't reckoned on this degree of response. We told him that it was a set-up but he wouldn't believe us. As far as he was concerned there was a gorilla on board and he wasn't moving until we were back in port.

He never forgave us for the trick.

It wasn't the first and I'm sure won't be the last surprise visitor on the *William Sampson*. One Hallowe'en night we had a young boy on board who'd been pestering us to let him come to sea for weeks and weeks. He was delighted to sit and listen to our talk in the galley, feeling like one of the men. Then I said nonchalantly that I'd heard the diver was back. The others just grunted as though this was nothing, but he couldn't resist asking what I meant. So I told him the story of the diver who was lost overboard in the very area we were fishing, and how from time to time he came back to haunt the boats. The boy was fascinated but not at all bothered by this, and the conversation turned to other matters. When we'd finished eating I asked him to go and get me a chain link from a locker up in the forepeak.

He hadn't noticed that our engineer John Wannell wasn't present for any of this talk of ghosts. John always carried a wetsuit on board in case he needed to go over the side to work on the propeller. A while before, we'd put him into his wetsuit and I'd wound a white bandage around his head before pulling the black helmet on over it. While we were in the galley he'd crept forward and hidden under a net in the chain locker up in the forepeak.

The boy went forward quite happily to this chain locker on his errand and climbed down through the tiny hatch which was just big enough to let a man through. When he disappeared from our view we all ran to peer over the edge.

While the boy was searching for my bit of chain, John reached out and grabbed his ankle. The boy glanced down, thinking he'd snagged his foot in some of the general debris littered across the deck, and shook his leg to free himself. Then John, who'd remained silent, moved under the net so that his white face suddenly became visible and he just moaned quietly.

The boy let out the loudest scream you've ever heard. In his hurry to get out of the locker he nearly pulled John's arm out of its socket and he ran aft hardly touching the deck, screaming all the way. We told him it was just a joke but he wouldn't speak to anyone for the rest of the trip.

Gutting fish is another activity full of possibilities for practical joking. One of my favourites was to take a cod or a ling and gut it very carefully through the gills so that there was no sign of the fish having been touched. On the next haul we'd throw it back in with the rest of the catch. From a vantage point you could then watch the man slit the belly and do a double take when he couldn't find the guts. The response never varied. He'd look down the mouth and then look around to see if anyone was watching him. Then he'd have another look in the belly, and probe about a bit. Making sure he was still unobserved he'd then throw it over the side, afraid to say anything to anyone about a fish which had been swimming around without any guts. You could see it going through his mind while he carried on gutting the rest of the catch, trying to work out how it could have been possible.

I suppose we all dream of finding something valuable in the nets which will change our lives. One of the crew on my nephew Stephen's boat kept going on about how he always looked carefully through the catch in case something valuable turned up. Sure enough one day there was a shout of excitement from the deck. He'd found his fortune at last, in the shape of a jewellery bag which had come aboard amongst the catch. Stephen watched from the wheelhouse as the man opened the small bag carefully, not daring to hope what it might contain. When he discovered the diamonds he looked like he was holding a million-pound pools cheque. There in his hands was the key to a Rolls Royce and his new lifestyle. No more of all this flogging himself to death every week out at sea. He rushed up to the wheelhouse to show them to Stephen, saying that they mustn't tell anyone. Stephen found a small piece of black rag to wrap the diamonds in and put them in a drawer in his cabin for safekeeping until they got into port. For the rest of the trip the man was in a daze, daydreaming of his untold wealth. By the time they came into the harbour he even had a taxi waiting to take him straight to a jewellers in Penzance to get them valued.

What he didn't know was that before they'd left Stephen had bought a kids' necklace in Woolworths, prized out the glass diamonds and put them in a jewel bag. Then he'd slipped them into the pile of fish as it came out of the net, where this deckhand found them as he searched through the sand and rubbish.

The jeweller must have wondered what was going on. Although they looked amazingly real to a casual layman's glance, under the magnification of his eyepiece they must have been easily revealed as nothing more than glass.

When he came back down the quay the boys pretended to be eager for information. But it was obvious what had happened. He'd lost the spring in his step and looked really dejected. In fact he looked as though he'd actually lost a million pounds. He was so depressed that to this day no one has had the heart to tell him what actually happened for fear of ending up in the harbour.

 FISHERMEN FROM ALL over the south-west have been up to London on a special train today to protest about this ridiculous new legislation the government's proposing. We stayed at sea, because I can't see the demonstration doing any good. The government want to protect fish stocks by limiting the number of days our boats can stay out at sea. We all know that some sort of conservation has to be started, but making our boats tie up in port is not the right method. The decrease in days at sea would only apply to British boats, while boats from other countries would be allowed to carry on as normal. It doesn't take too much of a genius to see that the gaps we leave will be filled by fleets from other countries, who will be able to sail into our empty waters to fish with no competition, while we're forced to stand back and watch. We're not going to protect any fish stocks unless we completely close off certain areas to fishing for a limited period.

The old boys in Newlyn say that before World War II fish stocks were being depleted alarmingly. Then fishing almost totally stopped during the war and those few years' rest were enough to let the ground recover. When they went out again there was so much fish around they hardly had to go outside the harbour to fill their boats up.

It doesn't seem too difficult to impose a total ban in something like a thirty square mile area of spawning grounds so that the fish would have an opportunity to breed and recover. But what's happening instead? By proposing to limit just us, our government is continuing a long tradition of not backing our own fishing industry against the rest of Europe. We saw it just before the European quotas were allocated. All the other European fleets inflated the amounts they claimed to be catching, knowing they would only be allowed to keep a proportion of that false quantity and therefore they would maintain the real level. In Britain we put down exactly what we were catching so our final share was less. All the time our neighbours have allowed for a growth in their industry while we've remained static at best.

The problem comes from the top. We have a minister of Agriculture *and* Fisheries, and yet we're second class citizens compared with farmers. You only have to look at the subsidies given to agriculture to see the favouritism. Our coastline and fishing grounds contain all the species anyone could dream of, everything from cod to hake to monkfish, so surely it's a resource worth protecting.

We saw this apathy on the part of our government when Iceland introduced a 200-mile exclusion zone during the cod war in the mid-Seventies. Yes, they sent some frigates up there, but they didn't fight it as hard as they should have done. Our minister negotiated a worse deal than the Icelanders were prepared to offer when it all started. Trawlers were scrapped; Hull and Grimsby were killed; and we saw an influx of men down in Newlyn looking for work. Now it's happening all over again.

Of course it's not the first crisis we've faced. There was a decline in Newlyn in the Seventies when the fish started to get scarce and we didn't have the size or power of ship to sail off any great distance. Then the beamers came in and suddenly the possibilities were opened up with boats which were many times more powerful. That option isn't open to us again.

In many ways the beamers were the worst thing that could have happened to Newlyn. They meant a bonanza for the first few years, but now they're destroying the very resource we rely on. It was much the same when the huge 200-foot purse seiners went around catching, in one shot, quantities which our whole fleet of small mackerel lining boats would have survived on for months.

The lack of fish makes our jobs more dangerous too. We have to go out into deeper water in rougher weather than any sensible person would consider safe, just to stay competitive. Each winter now there are two or three small boats lost just because they're pushing themselves to the limit and beyond. Something has to be done quickly before all the fishing grounds are destroyed by over-fishing, and more lives are lost in the hunt for those last few fish.

As the search for fish gets tougher I find myself respecting the creatures we're hunting more and more. Years ago we towed up a trawl that we recognized as one which had been lost off the Newlyn boat *Auchmore* six months previously. In the cod end was a huge conger eel, trapped but still alive. He must have survived by gobbling away at anything he could reach, because there were several sets of skate frames trapped in the cod end within his striking distance. With the net on the deck I had a look and said to this old conger, 'We'll undo the cod end, old boy, and have you out of there and overboard in a minute,' which we did. We cut him free and let him back into the sea. He'd survived that long he deserved to last a few more years, or at least have another chance until someone else caught him.

I suppose I've always been a bit soft like that, but I just can't stand to see something which looks dignified, and in good condition, being killed. If I see a lovely big turbot looking strong and healthy, I wonder to myself how long he's been swimming around down there before we've got our nets to him. And then I see the lads plunge the knife in and I'll think, 'I wish we hadn't caught you.' It's the same with any good-looking fish really. We sometimes get a large lobster or crayfish sitting on the deck looking wise and magnificent. I wonder to myself how many times he's shed his shell and survived being attacked, or managed to avoid being killed before we've come along scraping the seabed clean, and his days are over. There he'll sit looking proudly at us, the instruments of his downfall, and I've just had to go down on the deck to put him back in the sea. Not a popular move with the lads, but I placate them by pointing out that the big ones don't sell very well.

These feelings don't spoil my enjoyment of eating fish, mind you. Food is one of the few pleasures left on board – you couldn't avoid the subject here on the *William Sampson* if you tried. We enjoy experimenting with new fish recipes, taking advantage of all the varieties we catch. We made ratatouille yesterday, and tonight we took some left over hake, sprinkled some cheese on top and baked it. What a discovery.

My favourite catch from the point of view of immediate consumption has to be prawns. The simplest way to cook them is the best. Fill up a large saucepan with them, put an inch of water in the bottom, then steam them for a few minutes. Make sure they're not fully cooked, but are still slightly jelly-like, then it's easy to pull the flesh out of the shells. Put some oil and garlic in a pan and sauté the prawns. Then the best bit: eat them straight away with some brown bread. They are flippin' rich! Scallops cooked in the same way are fantastic. On shore I'll add some white wine when they're sautéed and finish them off under the grill with a little grated cheese on top.

When I was younger we always used to eat spider crabs on board, especially in September when they're full of meat and superb. Back then we couldn't sell them, but now they get exported as delicacies to Spain and France.

They're all pretty good cooks on board here. One of Graham's favourites is curried monkfish tail. I have to admit they're not my favourite fish, too many memories of years on deck gutting them. When you cut into a monkfish to clean it, the putrid stench is

terrible. They must eat all sorts of rubbish which makes them stink. Most of the stuff we call monkfish is really angler fish. It's an amazing creature, with its enormous gaping mouth and a small lure which it dangles in front like a fishing rod as it swims along. The real monkfish is a bit like a violin in shape, and we don't see many of them these days.

My other least favourite fish is haddock, for different reasons. I've found it difficult to look at them since there was a period a few years ago when I was on deck. We were catching masses of them, twenty to forty baskets a go, which is difficult to imagine now when we catch four baskets of fish in total each haul if we're lucky. I don't know if haddock eat sea urchins or what, but they're very gritty and when you gut them this grit gets between your fingers and you end up with haddock rash. Now I can't really face eating them because all I can think of is that rash.

Cod and turbot are other fish I have problems with eating because of the worms. You find them in the thin flap of the underbelly where the gut lays. They won't do you any damage because you cut the flap off, but I can't look at even clean ones without thinking about it.

There's no doubt that my favourite fish has to be Dover sole: filleted, skinned and baked in the oven with onion, salt, black pepper and water or wine. You just leave it to cook slowly, then make some white sauce with the juices which come out. That's wonderfully rich. Last time we were in Holland having some work done on the engine we had sole cooked in a style I'd not seen before which they called Sole Picasso. A huge whole grilled Dover sole, head and tail hanging over the plate, split down the middle, filled with tiny shrimps and surrounded with fresh strawberries, oranges, apple and peaches, all finely sliced. I'll tell you what, it looked like a Picasso painting as well.

Dover sole has a tough skin which you can't tear, and has a mouth shaped like a letter S lying on its side where it feeds off the bottom of the seabed. Lemon sole is a lighter colour, yellowy brown, and a very neat fish around the mouth which is round in shape. The biggest sole we landed was twenty-five inches from her head to the tip of her tail and thirteen inches across the widest part of her back. She was full of roe down one side which made her look bigger again. When we caught that off Pendeen, it was the biggest

Mitch skinning a Dover sole

133

one they'd seen on the market, and it was sold separately as a novelty.

One of our local fish is mackerel, but I'm sorry to say I'm not very fond of it – far too boney.

I don't particularly like ray or skate either. These relations of the shark remind me too much of my early days at sea when I was responsible for the morning fry-up. We'd eat fish for breakfast every day and sometimes have it in the evening as well. It was my job to go down to the fish room and get the gutted, but not filleted, ray and bring it back to the galley to clean it. It would have been left on the ice for a couple of days to get rid of the ammonia, but even then the smell and the slime were awful. Come the end I couldn't take it any more, so I used to cut the wings out, leaving them connected at the top like a little handbag. Then we'd tow them over the stern by these handles for a watch to get rid of the stink and the slime.

A relation of the shark which I do like is the dogfish. We traditionally sold great quantities of them on the market, but there are noticeably less now. You see them in fish and chip shops as rock salmon, because of the pink flesh. They don't look very appealing on the market because they're left in a very bloody condition so that the blood colours the flesh, but in fact it's a very good clean fish to eat. Its mouth is positioned in such a way that it has to bite chunks out of food rather than scavenging bits of anything off the bottom of the seabed. We've never caught many of them on beam trawlers, but even the smaller boats which target them are catching less today. I'm afraid I can't help thinking back to the hundreds of heavily pregnant females, full of pups, which we used to catch and kill. We didn't know any better at the time, but of course we caught so many then that the stocks have gone right down. If we catch a large female full of young pups these days I make sure we put it back in the water. I can't see the point of killing all the young: far better put the female back in the sea and let her produce another batch.

We have the ultimate in freshness of course, but you can tell just by looking at a fish if it's been hanging around for too long. The skin should be shiny and have a full range of colours and the eyes should be nice and sparkling. When a fish is not fresh you see the eyes go a sort of doughlike colour, a bit like Tony's after a night in the Ship Inn. Another sign to look out for are ice marks where the flesh has been bruised. In the old boats in which the fish was kept in large pounds, the weight of the mass of fish and ice used to bear down on the fish at the bottom and bruise them. We used to have lots of problems with melting ice, not so common now that most boats store their fish in crates within controlled refrigerated holds. You can still see it sometimes on the market when a chap has gone to sea a little short of ice and he's spread what he has around a bit too thinly. The fish aren't kept quite cold enough so they go black, and you end up with a black slime over them. They're not inedible by any means, but they just don't look so good or taste so fresh.

On our wet fish boats the gutted catch is kept just above zero, not frozen, so the texture and flavour is kept beautifully even when they're down in the ice room for eight or nine days. These days the methods used on large factory ships which catch, fillet, skin and freeze fish within an hour or two of being caught mean that even frozen fish can be pretty good. They won't have been out in the air more than an hour and most of them are processed without being touched by humans. Sometimes they can be better than some wet fish from trawlers which have been out ten days and not looked after their catch carefully.

The secret for frying any fish is very hot fat so that it sings when you put it in. Back when I was cabin boy I had to cook on a wretched coal stove, and stoking it to maintain a temperature high enough to keep the fat hot was terrible. Woe betide you if the fish wasn't cooked properly, with the flesh perfectly white. The old man would go bananas. I came close to hating the sight of fish at that time – cooking a big basket full of the stuff every day for seven big, very hungry men. The slightest fault when you brought the huge dish down meant trouble. Having to wait until they'd eaten and I'd finished cleaning the cabin always meant cold, greasy leftovers for me, which was not a recipe for continued enjoyment of the stuff.

There's one dish I love but am not allowed to cook at sea any more, fishcakes. Graham says that every time I cook them we have bad luck. I suppose he has a point: last time I'd just finished frying the first batch, and Mitch had taken two 'just to taste', when there was an almighty bang and the small winch engine blew up. The time before, we lost one of the nets. I still reckon they're worth the risk, though, they're so different from the ones you buy in shops. You grill any mixture of filleted and skinned white fish so that it's just starting to go a beautiful golden colour and is slightly crispy, chop some onions and sauté them until they're golden as well. Mix these together with an equal quantity of mashed potato, perhaps

Making fishcakes at home

a little parsley to add some colour, and a couple of raw eggs. Form them into balls and gently pat them into the traditional fishcake shape. Then just dip in seasoned flour, not breadcrumbs, and fry them. You end up with a beautiful coloured and flavoured fishcake.

All this talk of food has made me hungry. Time for a furtive visit to the galley – I might even risk making some fishcakes while Graham's turned in.

 AS THE FRENCH coast appeared in the early morning light I couldn't help wondering if I'd done the right thing talking my way into the trip. The promised week of sunshine and relaxation was already turning into anything but a holiday. I'd changed ships, leaving the *William Sampson* for the sixty-one-year-old trawler *Excellent*. I've worked on her several times over the years, but for this voyage the nets have been lashed to her sides as we were on our way to take part in a rally of historic ships in the Breton ports of Brest and Douarnenez.

Excellent was built for a fishing family in Scotland but used by the navy during the war, after which Old Man Willie Stevenson bought her to fish out of Newlyn. Willie would have approved of the way that his son, Billy, has become obsessed by reading and talking about the history of boats, their designs and working life, and the *Excellent* is the proof of his obsession. She last fished about three years ago and he's had his shore crew restore her specially for this trip. There is even a new galvanized bucket to go under the piece of wood which acts as a loo.

On board we have John Swan, the Stevensons' shore engineer; Roger Treneer, the shipwright; Peter Tonkin, a fishbuyer; and Michael Corin, another skipper. A real motley crew. One of the other skippers in Newlyn, Mervyn Mountjoy, was in charge and I was there purely for the ride, until I realized that only three of us were used to being at sea.

Far from sitting back with a cup of coffee relaxing, I ended up sharing a twelve-hour watch with Mervyn on the journey across. I don't work that hard when I'm fishing! The poor old girl needed helping all the way. Not far out of Newlyn harbour John had gone down into the engine room to coax the old engine along, and he never really emerged again until we got to France. I suppose she didn't do too badly considering her age and the fact that she hadn't been used for a while. The first major problem was when the bilge pumps packed up and the rising water level below threatened to swamp the ship. John pumped away by hand, calling up above the clatter of the old diesel, 'You remember that series *Boat* about the German U-boat?' I remembered the series but couldn't think why he was asking. 'Well it's just like that down here!'

Very appropriate since we were on our way to the site of the old U-boat pens in Brest. With all hands to the pumps we made

137

it, with most of the boat above the water. As the dockyard appeared we knew we wouldn't have to send out a Mayday call. The *Excellent* chugged her way through the fleet of tall ships, cutters and assorted craft which had already arrived from every port you could think of in Europe. There were supposed to be over a thousand vessels, mainly classic sailing boats, assembled here for the festival.

In our berth alongside the harbour walls we opened a few bottles of beer and looked at the impressive lines of the tall ship which was berthed alongside. We were moored with the powered working vessels: MFVs (Motor Fishing Vessels) just like us, some built during the war, and old tugs lovingly restored. The fleet of Little Ships on its way to Dunkirk must have looked very similar.

We were amazed to find out that over the next couple of days over a million people came out to visit the festival and although there were bands and entertainments not connected with the sea, most were there to see the boats. Why is it that the French are so keen on their maritime tradition while we couldn't really care less? We saw it in the fish restaurants along the harbour where people queued for hours to enjoy fantastic platters of fruits de mer served with great style, and probably containing lots of the fish which we'd caught in Newlyn but sent over here because no one at home would buy it.

We had a great bunch moored alongside us. On our starboard side an MFV from Dartmouth sailed by a father with his son and daughter, on our portside another MFV which had been cleverly converted into a charter boat. The crew of three had brought a group of people to visit the festival. Next to them was an MFV still in service with the navy in Plymouth. The Chief Petty Officers on board told us they were there as support boat to a navy sailing yacht crewed by officers which was taking part in the festival. After a few beers they said they were really there to make sure the officers didn't cock up the sailing or navigation, and generally to keep an eye on them!

On our third day we were joined by our BBC film crew who were to sail down from Brest with us. We set off for Douarnenez, about three hours sailing down the coast. Mervyn was anxious to get there because there was some dispute as to whether we would be able to moor alongside a harbour wall, or whether we would have to anchor off. One look at our rusting hook with no warp attached made it clear that we'd have to go for a harbour berth. None of us gave much hope for the ship if we had to lay at anchor.

An hour out of Brest, just as we were running past the old gun emplacements which I suppose would have guarded the U-boat pens, there was an almighty scream and a thump. I ran aft and almost fell over John's slumped body. At first I thought this was another wind-up. Then I saw the bloody gash on his forehead.

He was just conscious but so dazed he couldn't speak, so I lifted him up and carried him aft to the galley. He'd been up on the wheelhouse roof cleaning it in preparation for our entry to the second half of the festival when he'd stood up and been bashed by the spinning radar scanner. The force was so great that it threw him across the wheelhouse roof and he'd only just avoided going straight overboard by instinctively grabbing the first thing which came to hand. Then he'd crawled down the ladder and slumped on the deck.

Luckily there was some ice in the ice room where we'd been keeping the beer cool, and I managed to put some on what was now a huge bump. Then I made him a cup of hot sweet tea. By this time poor old John was shivering away and desperate to go to sleep, but we kept talking to him so he'd stay with us.

Mervyn radioed to ask for a fast boat to come out to pick him up, but the wonderful French coastguards weren't interested. This was on a day when over a thousand boats, many of them under twenty foot, were setting sail just behind us. It makes you appreciate our own rescue services. I can't imagine them refusing a request like that – they'd most likely have had rescue boats out and about as a precaution in any case.

We began to get worried about John. His lump was the size of a golfball and getting bigger. He was shivering more, and it was difficult to see how he could have got away without doing some sort of damage, concussion at the very least.

We were lucky: even with the old engine, *Excellent* could still move at a fairly good rate of knots.

The harbourmaster in Douarnenez ran down to try and stop us mooring, until we explained that we had an injured man aboard. We managed to get John up the ladder ashore, and even he laughed when, instead of the taxi we'd asked for, a red ambulance arrived complete with flashing lights, siren and a team of four ambulancemen, falling over themselves to help him into the back. It was just like the Keystone Cops.

The hospital was a surprise. Brand new, full of high tech equipment and apparently enough doctors and nurses to operate it all. John was whisked straight into a cubicle where he was

examined within minutes, then straight in for x-rays which appeared, processed, before he could be wheeled the fifty yards back to the cubicle. Another doctor immediately looked at these plates and gave him the all clear. This was all within the space of about twenty minutes from arriving at the door. As he was filling out a prescription for pain killers the doctor asked what we were doing in the port. When we explained that we were at the festival he pointed at John then asked knowingly, 'Drink?' much to John's disgust. He obviously didn't believe John's denial because he turned to us and told us to make sure he didn't have any drink tonight anyway.

The lads had to moor the trawler out off the harbour and just as we climbed back on board a huge caravel sailed past and dropped anchor. Looking through the binoculars I could see her name, the *Pinta*. By one of those strange coincidences I had spoken to her on the radio when we'd been out fishing off the Scillies last week. She'd been converted from an old French crabber and was now used mainly for film work. She'd just come back from South America where she and two sister ships had been involved in making two films about Columbus.

I hopped on board one of the small boats which were ferrying people around the fleet and went across to her. I didn't expect anyone to remember my radio call, but found that the mate I'd spoken to had even noted it in the ship's log. It was great to have the chance to look around the boat which I'd only seen across the water. It was a strange hybrid beast with all the modern navigation aids hidden behind false panels, making it look as though it had nothing but sail power. The mate told me that when all the sails were set she really moved along, far faster than by engine, which I could believe.

The highlight for me was climbing the old style rigging up the masts. I could imagine myself as a pirate boarding Spanish galleons, stealing their gold, taking their women. . . .

A tall ship at the Douarnenez festival

THE LADS HAVE left me alone today because I've been snapping at them over everything and anything. I caught Graham raising an eyebrow and rolling his eyes at Jiggy, 'The old boy can't take it!' he said with disgust, but I can't help it. Sophie went into Truro city hospital last night to have her tonsils out. The operation was at three o'clock this afternoon and I can't stop thinking about the poor little thing. We've never put her through anything like this before, always protected her from any physical pain as much as possible, so I almost feel as though I'm betraying her by letting her go into hospital. You hear so many stories of kids going in for operations and coming out damaged by something going wrong. I don't know what I'd do if anything happened to Sophie.

I keep thinking back to when I had my tonsils out when I was thirteen. They gave me a pre-med which was supposed to subdue me a bit, but it never made a bit of difference. I saw the first three go into theatre ahead of me, then come back and I was still fully awake. Even as they wheeled me down the corridor on the trolley I still didn't feel any different. Then they brought the rubber gas mask down on my face and enough was enough. I pushed it away shouting, 'I'm not having it.' I was so big and strong that I stopped them as well.

In the end they resorted to using a needle which I don't even remember coming out of my arm. The nurses said afterwards that they'd had to use a double dose of anaesthetic. The next thing I knew I was fighting for water and three people had to hold me down to stop me going to a tap.

I've never really got on with hospitals. A couple of years back I had terrible problems with my stomach. I would suddenly get such a bad pain that it would double me up for hours. It got so bad on one occasion that I only just managed to stop Nellie sending for an ambulance. When it happened at sea it wasn't much of a joke. The doctor sent me into hospital to have x-rays done, and I was convinced they thought it was cancer.

The night before I went in I had to take some tablets of a dye which would show up on the x-rays. I got into hospital, stood on the x-ray platform, held the two handles to keep still while the thing whirred a bit as they pressed a few buttons before they left the room. They came back in looking baffled. There was no sign of the dye on the film. They asked if I was sure I'd taken the tablets. I didn't bother to answer but I'm sure my look convinced them not to ask stupid questions again. They decided the only option was to send me home to take double the quantity.

I returned to the hospital and they went through the procedures again. This time they came back even more mystified, there was absolutely no trace of it. I knew they thought I was mucking around. They did loads of other tests, but gave up in the end saying there couldn't be anything wrong with me, which seemed to be a bit of a cop-out. Nellie reckons I must be bionic inside.

Mind you, I've had stomach problems since I was little. When I was three months old I had a major operation to cure something called pyloric stenosis, which is apparently quite common in baby boys. The outlet of the stomach is too narrow and food can't pass through. The scar from the operation stretches all the way across my stomach, which is quite a long way now.

Much later on in life I suffered from a hernia, which they operated on. I had so much fat that they had to cauterize the wound as they went along to stop the capillaries bleeding, so I didn't lose much blood. I came out of the operation and was brought around in the recovery room before being taken back to the ward where the other two who'd been done before me were snoring away. The nurse told me to go to sleep, but I lay there for a few minutes wide awake and getting totally bored. I decided to pull myself up by the strap hanging above the bed, got out and wandered into another ward to have a chat with a few people. The surgeon came in and stopped dead.

'What are you doing up?' he yelled. I told him I'd had a lie down for ten minutes but I couldn't stand it. He asked if I had anyone at home and told me I might as well go out a couple of days ahead of schedule. By the time I left, the nurses were having to bully the others into pulling themselves up and moving about a bit while I sauntered out carrying my bag. I still have another hernia, and if I tense my stomach you can see a great bulge where it's split open, but it doesn't bother me.

I suppose I'm just lucky to have always had a high pain threshold. As lads we'd go into the phone box, where they had those small mirrors, take a long darning needle and pierce our ears. We never bothered with anaesthetics or even ice cubes to deaden the pain.

When I was first at sea I had a pretty nasty accident when I was lining, quite a dangerous type of fishing. You have about ten miles of line with a hook hanging down off a yard long strop every two fathoms, around 4500 hooks in total. This line is broken into about thirty lengths and each length is coiled in a basket. You start by throwing out a marker buoy and one end of the line attached to an anchor. Then as the boat steams off, the line is pulled out of the basket. The hooks come out at a rate of about three a second and three men stand around baiting each one as they fly out. You have to be pretty quick to bait one hook a second. As each basket runs out, another member of the crew joins the end of the line in the old basket to the head of the line in the new one. The whole process takes about an hour, with hooks flying through the air the whole time.

The line has to be kept taut so it doesn't snag on anything on the seabed and Donald Turtle, who was the skipper on this trip, was well known for liking to keep his lines very tight. The line was whipping out over the stern and we were working away. We were about halfway through a basket when one of the hooks got caught in the fourth finger of my right hand. Within seconds the full strain of the taut line pulled the hook right through the joint. It was well and truly embedded, with the barb caught behind the tendons, and the whole weight of the line hanging on this one hook. They eased the power off and we were able to cut the yard long strop which the hook was on.

So then I was left with this hook about three inches long sticking through my joint. Hooks were always getting caught in people's flesh and normally you'd just pull them all the way through, but I couldn't do that because it had pierced the joint. I couldn't easily pull it back out the way it had gone in either because the barb was under my tendons. But it couldn't stay there.

There was nothing for it: I got one of the lads to take me aft and hold my hand down on a board. I pulled hard at the hook with a pair of pliers in an attempt to take the hook back out the way it had gone in. As I tugged away, the tendons were pulled down my hand until the barb tore through them, and they were left bunched together in my palm.

I think I would have been all right if the hook had been old. Unfortunately it was new, the lead coating infected the wound, and I ended up with lead poisoning. The hand swelled up like a balloon and my ring got stuck on my finger, cutting off the blood supply. The nearest land was the Isles of Scilly but the hospital there couldn't do anything so I had to jump on the helicopter and fly back to Penzance.

They had to use a special piece of gear which was like a curved tin opener with a spike on the end to cut the ring off. This damn spike dug into my finger while they moved the blade to and fro like an instrument of torture. I felt it nudging against the bone, as they kept turning it until the ring came apart. I've still got the scar, and the finger is bent almost double by the tension from the damaged tendons. I can only move it a few degrees.

Hooks can do a heck of a lot of damage. I've seen them through noses, cheeks, legs and they are so big and the barbs so vicious they can do terrible things. I was on a lining boat once with a big chap, Jack Williams from over Porthleven. He caught one in his palm, right through the fleshy part of his thumb, and he ended up hanging over the side with the full weight of the line held by this hook. His stretch was so wide that none of us could reach out to cut the strop. So there he stayed holding three miles of line by the flesh of one hand. The boat went full astern, but the tension was still on the line and his hand went whiter and whiter. Before we could do anything more there was a great bang and the hook just flew out taking most of his palm with it. The circulation came back and there was blood everywhere, but, do you know, that great big man just wrapped an old rag around his hand and went straight back to the line basket to start baiting again. There was no question of going into port for him.

All these memories of injuries are not really the best diversion to take my mind off Sophie's operation but I suppose if Sophie has the Nowell pain threshold she'll be fine. I can't wait to get in tomorrow to go and see her.

3 AUGUST

SOPHIE'S OPERATION WENT well. By the time I got into port and up to Truro she was awake, sleepy but talking, and didn't seem to be in too much discomfort. Now we're back at sea, fishing close to the Scillies. We ended up going in to St Mary's harbour to drop off David Secombe who has been with us for a few days taking photographs. It was his first time on a trawler and I've never seen anyone so relieved to see land. He said that he never imagined it would be possible to feel so ill. He spent most of the time in his bunk, or hanging over the side, coming up looking like a ghost to take the odd photo now and again. I'm sure Graham's sarcastic running commentary didn't help.

It was a good job we were allowed into the Scillies. Unfortunately some Newlyn netters went in there a while back, had too much to drink and caused a bit of trouble in the harbour, playing music loudly on their boats in the middle of the night, which spoilt it for everyone for a while. It's all been resolved now and Newlyn boats are allowed back in to a place which has many happy memories.

When I was trawling before the days of the three and later twelve mile limits we used to dodge around the islands, sneaking in and out of the rocks looking for the places where the fish hide. There was one particular bank which was so close to the shore that you could throw a stone on to the land from it. Sometimes we could even read the newspaper headlines off the papers of tourists sitting on the beach. It was a great place for catching lovely big rays and massive plaice with spots as big as a two bob bit. It had never been touched by trawlers like ours, only a few liners from the islands.

The first time we hauled after we'd discovered the patch we couldn't believe our luck. The net came out of the water full of all this lovely clean, sweet smelling seaweed, all beautiful rich colours, you could almost eat it. Then the net came over the rail and it was absolutely bursting, bulging with fish. When we undid the cod end, that much fish came out it spread across the deck like water. Standing in one position without moving your feet on the deck you could fill up nine baskets with lovely big clean fish.

A stop-over in the Scillies

The Scillies was a great area to fish around and we made quite a few friends during our brief visits. If the weather was bad or we just wanted a break we'd go in, moor up, and leap ashore for a barbecue or an evening in The Mermaid at the end of the quay. We could fish close enough to the islands to make a quick trip ashore possible.

When we were over there we'd quite often go into the Co-op shop to get a sub, which we'd pay back at the Co-op in Newlyn. Mitch once went into the Scillies for bad weather and had no cash, so out came the scallops, and they were sold on the quay. In the end people were queuing up in cars. The locals went away with cheap scallops and Mitch and the boys had a few pounds for a pint.

For quite a while brother Frankie and I sailed with a skipper from Dartmouth who was Plymouth Brethren, so wouldn't be at sea on a Sunday. We used to try and make sure we were off the Scillies of a Saturday night at around nine or ten o'clock so we could have the last haul and make for St Mary's to have Sunday ashore there. It was a really nice way to work. This was in the days when the Scillonian ferry didn't run on Sundays, nor did the helicopters, so you had the jetty to yourself, and there were no hoards of day visitors. The islands were cut off for twenty-four hours. There was a chap there who even used to keep the previous Sunday's papers, unread, to be able to enjoy them the following week.

We had one great Saturday night when we went ashore and met up with a gang from one of the campsites. We sat around drinking beer until about five in the morning then went back down to the boat. There was a large skylight in the sleeping quarters which we opened up and this chap sat with his head sticking out playing a guitar until dawn. It was like being on holiday.

An islander called Leslie Forward often used to row out in his small punt to meet us as we towed along, bringing fresh vegetables with him from his garden: new potatoes with the dark Scillies soil still on them, a turnip or cabbage, which we'd exchange for a bag of fish. I can see him now wearing a trilby hat, rowing like hell to catch us, the sweat dripping off him. If he came out in the evening he'd bring out a couple of bottles of beer as well. The type of side-winder trawler we were working then was a lot less dangerous than today's beamers or even long liners, so we'd break our rule of not drinking at sea. He'd spend a tow with us, his rowing boat trailing behind us as we towed in a huge circle. We'd have a good old yarn, then as we towed in close, he'd push himself off and row ashore

148

shouting, 'See you tomorrow if you're here!' over his shoulder, his trilby hat bobbing away in our wake.

Sure enough if we were still around the next morning we'd see the hat coming towards us and he'd climb aboard in time to share the fish breakfast which we always used to cook. These visits were especially good when he brought out the papers. It was great to be able to read the Isles of Scilly edition of *The Cornishman*, or even yesterday's national papers.

This was in the days before we had television on board; we didn't even have VHF radio to speak to other boats. In fact we only had a big high frequency radio to pick up the weather forecasts and for emergencies. You didn't dare tune the set to anything else, the skipper would go mad – it was only there for his official use. So the possibility of reading a bit of news caused great excitement.

It was a lot more fun fishing then. We'd spend hours talking to each other instead of just sitting vacantly in front of the television. We would end up ashore in different places. Dunmore East in Ireland was a favourite, where we'd go in with all the herring boats, and have many a do in the pub with an old boy playing a fiddle in the corner.

I'm sure it's not just selective memory making it seem more fun, we didn't have anything like the hassles we do now. We had no MAFF chasing us, or limits on what we caught. Everyone seemed to enjoy themselves more. On our way back into Newlyn in the summer we'd quite often stop off in Lamorna Cove just south along the coast from Newlyn and anchor up with a couple of other trawlers for a couple of hours so that all hands could have a swim in the beautiful clear water. Our boss would have gone spare if he'd known.

One week we were there when a fisherman from Penberth Cove came around in his small boat with a party of holidaymakers who snapped away at us with their cameras. I shouted across for him to be sure to send me a set of the photographs. A couple of weeks later there was a radio message that there were some pictures waiting for me back in the harbour. The stupid so and so had sent them to the office. I thought, there'll be a row now! But when I walked in there was just great laughter from all the girls. I know we're not exactly Newlyn's answer to the Chippendales, but the comments about beached whales were uncalled for. I don't think the boss could bring himself to have a go at us, once he saw how much the girls had mocked us!

 I'VE BEEN EXCITED all day today. Nellie's bought a little twenty foot open boat, the type we call toshers. Her dad left her some money, and she thought it would be good to buy something with it to keep me out of trouble.

We'd been half-heartedly looking for one for a while, but they've all been too expensive for their condition. Then I saw an advert in the local paper with a price I couldn't believe – it was frighteningly cheap. When I spoke to the chap he explained that he's a builder and used the boat for the odd bit of mackerel lining in the evenings, but with the state of the building business as it is he's had a few cashflow problems, so needed to sell her quickly.

We arranged to meet the following evening in Hayle, just round the coast from St Ives. As we waited for the boat to come in I wasn't too hopeful; every trip to look at a boat had been a disappointment so far. I saw a beautiful little white tosher come up towards the harbour, and said to Nell how it was a pity we couldn't find one like that: it was immaculate, but it would be too expensive for us. I couldn't believe it when this boat stopped in front of us and moored exactly where we'd arranged to meet.

The Gods were sending us encouragement because it happened to be Nell's dad's birthday. The next good omen was difficult to believe. I saw that the name of the boat was *Sheila Jan*. Nell's real name is Sheila, so that was that.

We took her over to Newlyn today and she's on a mooring by the lifeboat. When I took her for a spin around the harbour it was just like stepping back to my youth when I used to go out in my dad's tosher. I met Brother, just about to go to sea, and asked him if it reminded him of the days we used to muck about around the harbour. All he could think of was the time I was about eight years old when he and a friend took me out in the boat with strict instructions from Mother to look after me. When they got into the middle of the harbour he threw me in and sculled away laughing.

I can't wait to spend the odd evening in *Sheila Jan*, pottering around looking for a few mackerel out in the bay with Sophie, Nell and Shevie. It will be a great way to relax.

I've never been good at hobbies, partly because with only two days ashore at a time it's hard to keep anything going. I've tried everything from growing tomatoes to calligraphy. I like to buy all the best gear, but the new interest falls by the wayside very quickly.

Horse riding was about the only thing I kept up for a while. I started one year after Paul Feast, a day in November which traditionally celebrated the end of the pilchard driving season and the change to lining for mackerel. The boats would come in, take their nets off, paint everything up and kit themselves out with lines. In the village of Paul, up above Newlyn, the highlight of the celebrations was the hunt. This particular year I was up there watching and thought to myself, that's what I'd like to do, so went out and bought a horse complete with all the gear. I called her Southern Comfort because that was what I was drinking at the time, and I found there was nothing better than coming in from sea and going off for a ride across the fields.

One day a sign went up on the pier saying 'No Dogs', part of yet another set of rules to do with hygiene. I hate being told what to do so much I thought I'd see what I could get away with. So I rode the horse down the pier, saying to the harbour master as I rode past that the sign only forbade dogs. Unfortunately I only got halfway down when she got frightened by the movement of the boats and shied up, so I took her across the road, tied her up outside the pub and went in for a pint.

We seemed to spend more and more time at sea and less on land, and it became very expensive to keep her in the stables, so in the end Southern Comfort had to go.

Then I bought a bike and would cycle down to the harbour to go to sea. One day I came down and discovered that we weren't going out because of bad weather which made me so mad that I threw the bike into the harbour. Later on Nellie bought me another one, and I used it a few times to cycle to the pub. I'd have a few beers, phone Nellie to collect me, and put the bike in the car boot. I got fed up with the fact that this thing only had three gears and used to be a devil to get up the hills. So after I'd had a few pints one night I decided to leave it at the pub, where it stayed for years. It may even be there still.

I can only think that I haven't been successful in taking up hobbies because by the time you come in from sea you're just too knackered. When I was a kid we were always up to something. We had dens all over the quarry, hewn out of the huge piles of sand they used for making bricks. One type went a bit like sandstone and was so hard you could cut into it with a shovel. We'd make a tunnel using scaffold poles and corrugated iron to reinforce the roof, making it so strong that the lorries used to drive across the top. From the outside you couldn't tell there was anything there, but we'd excavate an alcove and put a candle in it, then sit around making catapults and exchanging stories. All the kids had these hideouts and when we weren't in the harbour we'd be playing there.

It was the time when entertainment and toys were all home made, and much the better for it. I can remember the excitement building up just before Christmas one year when I knew my old dad had spent months making me a wooden wheelbarrow. Although it wasn't a surprise when he actually gave it to me I just loved it. Jiggy was saying the same thing in the galley the other day. His dad was a chippie in the merchant navy and one year he made Jiggy a wooden rocking horse out of one block of wood. He was a talented man: the barber in Mousehole used to have a set of wooden chain links he'd made out of one piece of wood. I feel sorry for the kids today who end up with plastic toys bought in shops and don't do anything but sit in front of the television or play computer games.

We'd been brought up learning to amuse ourselves. It was a good old time for having a lark, and even if it got us into trouble it was usually fairly innocuous. I was given a dufflecoat once which was so big that it came down to my ankles, so I thought for a bit of a laugh I'd dress up in it with a bowler hat and a pair of dark glasses and walk down through town to see if anyone recognized me. As I made my way down the hill I cut off a branch from a May tree and used my pocket knife to strip most of the bark off so that it was white, which was how we made our swords. I arrived at the bridge and waited for a gap in the traffic so I could cross. It's a busy bottleneck in the village where the cars scream past, but suddenly they stopped, in both directions. I couldn't believe it, then I realized what had happened. My sword looked like a white stick. I couldn't run across because it would make those people feel stupid or conned, so I took my time, tapping as I went. I'd never intended this but I had to carry on along the harbour until I was out of sight. Then I saw Billy Stevenson, who opened the door for me as I went into the office. As I passed him I started to grizzle. He came running after me, furious, 'You might be like that one day.' I tried to tell him I'd never even meant to impersonate a blind person, it had simply happened – but he wouldn't listen.

I must admit that motoring around today in the new little tosher *Sheila Jan* made me feel a bit like a big kid again. We used to count how many minutes were left to the end of school every day, looking forward to rushing down to the harbour. I'm sure I'll be the same out at sea now, looking forward to coming in so I can muck about in her.

 I'VE JUST HEARD on the news that a boat's been arrested for smuggling drugs a few miles up the coast. There seems to have been a lot of activity lately down around this area, even one of the pubs in town was raided for drugs the other day, although I don't think they found anything. Mind you, it has been known for one or two of the local netter boys to smoke something which has a slightly different smell from any tobacco you can buy in the shops. If any of my lot tried it at sea they'd be out on their ears, although I can't imagine Bobby or Jiggy smoking dope! I tried the stuff myself when I was young, the odd roll-up of grass, but I never thought much of it; I always found the effects pretty unsociable really. People became very introverted, quiet and altogether boring.

You can't fish in Cornwall and be too much a stranger to modern day smuggling, it's such a popular area for it. Brother Frank came in from sea once and had to move a yacht away from the harbour wall so that he could berth. The following day he woke up to hear people swarming over his deck and on to the yacht, and when he looked they were Customs men. They took the yacht into Penzance, pulled her apart and found £3,000,000 worth of cocaine wrapped around the engine.

Trawlers are pulling the stuff up all the time. One skipper was arrested and taken in by the police because his crew had trawled up a bale of drugs while he was turned in and had hidden it away. He spent a trip with all this stuff stacked around the boat drying out, without knowing anything about it. I think the Customs heard about it when the youngsters tried to sell the stuff ashore, and they pounced. The skipper got off the charges and he sacked the whole crew.

I was very nearly thrown into prison for drug smuggling once. We'd had a long hard week at sea, landed the catch and gone straight back out again, setting off from Newlyn to speed around the coast towards St Ives where we would start fishing. We were all so tired that I left Mitch on watch, put a cross on the chart for him to steer for and told him to come and turn us out when we got to the spot.

We arrived, turned out and shot the trawls. Despite being all in we forced ourselves to work for four nights around the area and then went back into harbour to land again. We went in through the gaps just as the early morning mist started to clear and as we moored up at the end of the pier I noticed a Landrover parked on the end of the quay, which was unusual at that hour. As we berthed, out jumped what seemed like an endless line of men. They were led by a neat-looking chap in a tweed jacket, carrying a small briefcase under his arm. He shouted across, 'Coming aboard, skipper!' and before being invited leapt on to the deck and climbed up into the wheelhouse. It was then that I noticed the other men were in HM Customs uniforms and were carrying torches, and mirrors on the end of long rods. They were swarming all over the boat by the time he was up alongside me.

'Well, what can we do for you?'

'We've been waiting for you for four days,' he replied, wiping the oil from his hands on a clean handkerchief.

I could hear his men all over the boat, pulling things out and looking behind and under just about everything, discovering things we'd forgotten we had on board. I couldn't imagine what it might have been about and why they'd picked on us.

'Can I look at your chart, skipper?'

Still no clue as to what he was after. He opened up his case and pulled out a matching chart of his own. He spent a couple of minutes comparing his with mine and then straightened up, looking pleased with himself. 'What's this mark here?' he asked, pointing at the cross I'd drawn to show the crewman where to head for. I explained that it was where we'd started fishing the first night out. His tone became more formal and stiff. 'Have you got any drugs aboard?'

'All in the medicine chest, the morphine and so on.'

'No, no, anything else?'

I was beginning to get a bit mad now. We'd been working so hard we could have done without this Newlyn version of the Spanish Inquisition. His men had pulled everything out and there couldn't have been an inch of the boat they hadn't poked or prodded. So I asked him what it was all about.

'You've been alongside a boat that's just come from Jamaica.'

Well this was news to me. I'd only seen a couple of other fishing boats, but sure enough the chap produced a black and white photograph taken from the air showing us pulling away from a large white cargo ship.

He explained that a Nimrod surveillance plane had been flying overhead four days earlier and had seen us near this banana boat, apparently steaming away from it having been alongside. They thought it looked suspicious and had reported it to the customs. There is a well known way of smuggling – called coopering – in which a small boat like a fishing boat or a yacht will meet a larger ship out at sea and transfer parcels of drugs. They then land them in their home port where they're not under any suspicion and can simply walk along the quay with their parcels. It would be so easy, any of us could easily bring a wad of drugs ashore whenever we landed, especially now that they're cutting back on the number of customs men.

Even though I knew we'd nothing dodgy aboard it was a nasty feeling to see what was apparently undeniable photographic evidence of just such a transfer. It did indeed look just as if we were pulling away from the large ship.

I called the crew up to the wheelhouse, showed them the photograph and said I wanted to know what was going on. Mitch looked at it and shrugged his shoulders. 'We nearly ran into that damn thing!'

He explained that while he'd been on watch and I was turned in, that huge white cargo ship of about 10,000 tons had suddenly stopped, right in our path of towing. He must have then realized he was going to get in our way and gone hard astern, as Mitch had to turn hard to port to avoid a collision. At this moment the plane spotted us and took what looked like an incriminating photograph.

I was getting madder by the minute and the customs chap was lucky to get away without being whacked, I can tell you. He'd been waiting night and day and now had all his little runners ferreting around, so he was wound up like a spring as well. He was still adamant that we'd been up to something, especially with the evidence of the cross on the chart. He was obviously an orderly, precise man, who wasn't going to be happy with any untidy outcome.

I was getting worried, because I reckoned if it went to court with a jury we'd have been in trouble. Who'd have believed me against the apparent evidence of the photograph?

Then I had another good look at the picture, and there was the proof I needed. You could just see our warps being towed behind us at an angle which meant we had to be fishing, so there was no way we would have been able to stop alongside the ship. The chap in the tweed jacket became slightly less officious and looked at the photo himself. At the same time one of his men came up to the bridge and said that they'd found nothing, and the poor chap was suddenly deflated. What we didn't know until later was that there had been another team of customs men at Barry in

Wales, waiting for the banana boat on the strength of a tip-off, so they had a lot riding on it.

Eventually we managed to convince him that it was quite routine for the person on watch not to wake the skipper when we found ourselves closer to another vessel than we'd like to be, because if he did we'd never get any kip! Looking really dejected, the little chap ordered his customs men back into the Landrover and they were gone. They left us with one old wellie, a sock and a packet of biscuits which we'd lost about five years previously.

Mind you, smuggling must be exciting, not so much today when they're dealing in hard drugs, but back when it was purely spirits or wine, and it was almost an acceptable occupation. Some of the old squires round here did pretty well out of the business. They were supplied with barrels and barrels of claret or brandy and were probably the worst culprits of the lot. Even some of the magistrates and vicars were quite prepared to turn a blind eye, as long as they got their booze. No wonder all the gentry had such bad gout a century ago.

I can see myself as a smuggler, out there in a fishing smack, running booze: all the barrels tied around the hull of the boat, weights and lines attached ready to cut them loose and let them drop to the seabed if the sails of the customs cutter were sighted. Then there'd be the fast escape, to return another day, find the small marker float, and pick up the contraband. And at the end of the voyage, the excitement of landing on a dark windy night, struggling through the surf towards the beach with the barrels, and an exhilarating climb up the cliffs, stopping and listening every few yards, waiting for the shout to go up.

The living must have been hard but the rewards great, a bit different from fishing today. I'm sure if I'd been born a century or so earlier I would have ended up a smuggler, it has such a strong appeal to me.

———————————

TODAY WAS ABOUT the only fine day all summer, which was lucky because it was the Newlyn fish festival. It's only the second time it's been held, but thousands of people turned up to wander around looking at the fish displays, craft stalls and of course the boats. I went over with Nell and Sophie and had a good old time wandering around. Billy Stevenson had opened up a couple of trawlers to the public, and had a display of some of the thousands of photographs he's taken over the years. He's got a room full of them at his house, a picture of nearly every boat that's been into Newlyn harbour. I said to him that when I'm out at sea I'm master of all I survey, and wondered if he feels the same when he looks out of his window at the harbour he's helped create. 'I do, and when I see you lot I wonder if I've done the right thing!'

He's a funny old boy really. To look at him in his shoes which flap at the toe, and glasses which have been mended with a couple of rivets through the bridge, you wouldn't take him for a millionaire and a member of a family who've built up the largest fleet of trawlers in the country. Yet all the Newlyn property which is painted cream and black as well as all the boats along the old pier in their green and white colours are evidence of the size of the business. Newlyn *is* the Stevenson family: for four generations they have influenced most areas of the town's life and there's no doubt in my mind that it would have died long ago without the family's push. I'm sure their interest will continue with Billy and Tony's children, who look set to take the family concern forward into the next century.

Mind you, you don't get to that position without being tough. Many people have fallen out with the family over the years, including me on several occasions. On the other hand I know of many unsung cases where the Stevensons have helped individuals when they'd no need to and where there was little chance of getting anything back.

I've worked for the Stevensons nearly all the time I've been a skipper. Billy and I have had our ups and downs over the years. I've been sacked a few times, but we've always made it up. Our disagreements tend to be on a more lighthearted basis now. He's

OVERLEAF With Billy Stevenson

157

always loved to make a bet with me, and though it's usually only for a fiver he always takes it very seriously. The only area it's never worth arguing over is where any historical detail is concerned since he's a walking encyclopedia of fishing knowledge, but I love to have a gentle jab at him in other ways to get him riled.

Back in 1982 I decided to go back to sea between Christmas and New Year which was unusual. I had a feeling we were going to do well and I said this to Billy, knowing that he could never resist a bet. He said that we wouldn't make £3000, but if we did he'd buy me a bottle of whisky, to which I joked that I only drink brandy. Anyway we returned and made a record amount of money from one catch, something like £6600. I was on my way down the pier when he pulled up in his old Triumph Dolomite. 'Well, what did you make?' With great relish I told him six and a half. 'You're having me on.' I showed him the auction slip and he just grunted.

Later he came back down, opened the glove compartment of the car and pulled out a miniature bottle of brandy which was his idea of a joke. I said I wanted the full amount. So later he came back and thrust a bag into my hand, saying that Enid, his wife, had been into an off-licence and bought me a bottle. This was quite a triumph for me because she didn't drink and quite likely had never been in an off-licence before. When I opened the bag there was my prize, half a bottle. It was just like Billy to have the last word.

A few weeks later I was down on the quay mending nets one Sunday morning when he walked along with two of his pals. I looked up at him while I carried on working away at the nets.

'There's one thing you'll never do as long as you live,' I said.

'What's that then?' he replied, immediately on the defensive.

'Mend nets like this.'

I could see I'd hit the spot. He'd been studying me as I'd kept working away, hands flashing.

I heard later that for three months after that he'd spent every evening up at the store with Jimmy the French learning how to mend nets.

Next time he came down the quay when I was working on the nets I knew he'd want me to make a comment which would give him the opportunity to say 'That's where you're wrong!' so that he could show me his newly acquired net-mending skills.

As he came closer I put the net down, took up a steel hawser and started splicing it. As he approached I looked up. 'This is one thing you'll never do as long as you live.' I expected him to at least swear at me or laugh, but he didn't even show a flicker of anger or surprise – just stood there with his hands behind his back looking at me.

I was the one who was surprised when I discovered that Billy had gone straight back up to the net store and spent the next few months learning to splice steel hawsers!

To this day I've never said anything to him about any of it, and he hasn't mentioned it to me either. He's a strong-minded person to say the least.

There was another occasion when storms were forecast. All the skippers came down the quay, had a discussion and decided we weren't going out to sea, so I sent the boys home. Next morning I came down and nearly all the fleet had gone. I never discovered why they'd gone without saying anything. It was in the days when we stuck together, so perhaps it was someone's idea of a joke. I knew there would be trouble now from Billy, who would be annoyed that I was still in port, not earning him money like the other boats were.

I went aboard, and was in my cabin getting ready to go to sea when a youngster who was sailing with us came in behind me. 'Where's the Decca gone then, Rog?' It took a moment to register that there was a space where the only navigation aid we had should have been. I thought at first that we'd been burgled, then I asked around on the quay and sheepishly the shore gang revealed the truth. Billy had ordered the electrician down to the boat to take it out.

He wanted to punish me for not going to sea like the others had done, but he knew that if he simply told me to stay in I would have ignored him. He also realized that without the Decca we'd have no way of navigating and I wouldn't be able to leave harbour. This was the ultimate punishment to his mind. However he hadn't correctly predicted the effect on the crew. I watched his bewildered face as all hands went up the harbour laughing and joking. What he hadn't worked out was that they were more than happy to be on shore for another day and he was the loser because his boat wasn't earning him any money. For once I had the last laugh.

———————————

 I'VE JUST RECEIVED an unwelcome but expected letter from Holland. A few weeks back we were up in the North Sea fishing and went into Stellendam to land our catch. We were in the harbour moored up alongside some other trawlers, waiting for some repair work to be finished so we could sail back south, when suddenly there was the sound of a siren, and people leaping all over the boats. A policeman turned up in my cabin, complete with gun, which always makes me a bit twitchy, and wanted to know if we'd lost any oil. They have spotter planes which fly over Dutch waters looking for any illegal dumping at sea or in port, and as a result their harbours are spotless and a delight to work in. The policeman explained that when the plane flew over that day it had seen a large patch of oil coming from our group of moored boats.

In Newlyn people empty their bilges out into the harbour; there's the occasional diesel spill and no one takes much notice. This oily muck covers the harbour walls and all the ladders, making it very hard to get ashore without getting covered in the stuff, and the place is filthy. It makes me mad, and I have every sympathy with the Dutch preoccupation with keeping their harbours spotless.

I knew that we hadn't thrown any oil overboard in Stellendam, but they had a brief look around the boat anyway. They couldn't find anything and boarded the next boat. After a while they returned and said that they'd narrowed it down to our boat, and this time had a really thorough search. Graham looked with them, but couldn't find any problems in the obvious places. Then blow me if in a virtually inaccessible corner they didn't find that one of our fuel tank breather pipes was completely corroded and diesel was leaking straight out over the side. This is a major crime in Holland and quite honestly I was surprised not to be taken off in handcuffs and thrown into jail there and then.

The letter this morning said that there would be a hearing in a few weeks' time and listed the different fines which could be imposed, so I'll just have to wait and see. The only consolation I have is that it hadn't been done deliberately, and that it was hardly as bad as the experience we had of an oil slick a few years back.

I'd been invited to a wedding so I went into Newlyn to have my hair cut. While the barber was snipping away he said to me that

he'd heard a coaster had gone on the rocks off Land's End and
they'd taken thirty or so people off her. I thought it sounded a bit
larger than a coaster with that many people on board. On my way
home I stopped off at the harbour to hear the latest news of this
vessel and it did indeed turn out to be a bit more than the barber
had thought. The date was 18 March 1967 and the ship was called
the *Torrey Canyon*.

Nearly 1000 feet long, and full with over 100,000 tons of crude
oil, she was en route from Kuwait to Milford Haven. Afraid of
missing high tide at Milford, the skipper decided to take a short
cut between the Isles of Scilly and Land's End which would save
him twenty-nine minutes. It was a costly decision; he struck the
Seven Stones Reef.

We went out to sea a couple of days later on our next fishing
trip. Our skipper said that if we made £1000 he'd buy us a bottle
of champagne. Within six days we'd filled the boat up, there was
that much fish around. When we came in we made £1300, more
than twice as much as normal. Mousehole's Ship Inn was emptied
of champagne, after we'd drunk four or five bottles of brandy.
None of us were very well the next day.

During those few days we'd been out, the *Torrey Canyon*'s oil
had gushed into the sea, causing an oil slick thirty-five miles long
and fifteen miles wide and it had become a major incident.

Most of the boats in the harbour were commandeered to spray
detergent on the slick. We heard from some of the other lads that
it was pretty easy work, but we didn't want to get involved in it
because we wanted a couple of days off, and we also felt we were
on a good run. So we kept our heads down, and then snuck out to
sea again before anyone could nab us. In the end we were one of
only two trawlers working in the south-west.

Newlyn was a strange place to be: not like a fishing port at all.
All the trawls were taken ashore and the boats steamed off to
Falmouth to pick up the detergent spraying gear. It was a huge
operation with special AA road signs pointing towards the harbour
saying 'Torrey Canyon Operation' as though it was a tourist
attraction. Drums and drums of detergent were lined up along the
quay and a big cleaning centre was set up at the top of the pier to
clean oil off the men's special overalls.

The trawlers carried the drums lashed around their decks and
at first it was sprayed across the oil, but this didn't work well. In
the end it was just tipped by the barrel-load on to the decks where
it ran out through the scuppers; the movement of the boat through

the water helped break up the oil. They got through 25,000,000 gallons of the stuff by the time it was over. The empty drums were put up on Tredavoe Hill above Newlyn. On a still night, even this far on, there's a sweet soapy smell which drifts across from where the last drops of the detergent soaked into the ground.

We steamed off to see the *Torrey Canyon* one day, sailing through the pollution which was a very strange experience. The boat felt very sluggish and there was no wash or wake as we moved through the thick brown treacly oil. It made the sea unnaturally flat, as though it was moving in slow motion, and you couldn't get away from the overpowering stench of crude oil. The *Torrey Canyon* just lay there very still in the water, a monster deprived of all its power. They resorted to all manner of attempts to disperse what was left of the tanker and its cargo. In the end the RAF and the Fleet Air Arm bombed it over a period of three days, which was spectacular, but I seem to remember that they missed on the first few runs.

Because of the flood of the tide, the oil was coming up towards Land's End and forking out. Some came into Mount's Bay, the rest was pushed up the north coast. Everywhere we went we saw thousands of seabirds covered in oil, and I wished we'd had a gun on board so I could have put them out of their misery. We had to be careful where we fished because of the oil, but you could smell it long before you could see it so we managed to discover enough clean areas. I have to say we made some money during that time.

The captain of the *Torrey Canyon* said that the strong currents took him off course and when he came to make the turn between the Scillies and the Seven Stones a lever on the steering control box was in neutral and the seconds lost fiddling with it were fatal. The ship couldn't be stopped in under three miles and it crashed into the reef. The skipper has been a broken man since.

A year or so after the disaster some marine scientists in Plymouth claimed that the detergent used was doing more harm to the sea life than the oil itself, and that the French method of using chalk to sink the oil had been more successful. We noticed that wherever detergent was used everything died, but I'm pleased to say that a quarter of a century later it's starting to come back. There are even a few shrimps in the harbour again.

————————

EVERY DAY OUT here at sea we get seagulls perching on the bow rail, heads pointing into the wind, bobbing in unison like a set of live weather vanes. It's quite a laugh watching the young birds attempt to imitate their elders' landing techniques, usually unsuccessfully, like trainee pilots landing harrier jump jets on an aircraft carrier. These birds are said to be the souls of dead skippers revisiting the ships.

Whenever a one-legged bird joins us someone will say, 'Good morning, Nicky,' out of respect for my old dad, Nicholas George Kennard Nowell. My Old Man was a fishing skipper in Newlyn, having started at sea on the battleship *Cornopus* in the First World War. During his time on her he fought in the first battle of the Falklands and the Dardanelles. After the war he went into the merchant navy and was sailing off Cuba when his leg was badly burnt in a fire aboard the ship. He was kept in Cuba for eighteen months while they tried to save his leg, but the treatment was unsuccessful and it was amputated.

When he was invalided out of the navy Nicky came back to Newlyn in a yacht on which he lived for years before moving into a house on the old quay. He ruined the yacht, apparently, by cutting out a piece of the forepeak to use it for pilchard driving. Then he bought a little tosher, a small open mackerel boat, and spent the rest of his days playing around with fishing. It was never really a great business with him; he just went out to catch a few fish to feed us and sold the surplus.

One year when Dad's tosher had seen the end of its days, most of the wooden hull having been repaired with lead sheeting, he decided to give us kids a show. On Guy Fawkes night he took the boat out to sea along Penzance promenade and set light to it. It was like a Viking funeral.

He came from a strong family. His brother was an enormous man in size and spirit by all accounts. When the Penlee lifeboat station was being built people would go across just to watch Uncle at work carrying three bags of cement, one under each arm, and one across his shoulders. He was quite a legend. But he was sent to France during World War I where he was shot by a sniper. When I see his name on the cenotaph right outside the seaman's mission I think about what it must have been like for him to leave the tiny fishing village of Newlyn and end up in the horror of the trenches.

Uncle's death gave the Old Man a real hatred of guns. Brother Frank bought an air pistol when he was about thirteen, which was a great secret because of the absolute ban on guns in our household. There was an old dear who lived alongside us, a proper old dragon, and an ugly old bugger really. She was always finding fault with us kids and we hated her. One day I saw my opportunity to get my own back when she was out in her garden hanging out washing. I took Frank's airgun from its hiding place, crept up to the hedge and waited as she struggled with the big tub of clothes. I lined up the sights on her great fat behind, chose my moment and caught her in the rump good and proper. It was a bit like Albert Finney in *Saturday Night and Sunday Morning* when he fired an airgun at that old woman's back. She leapt up in the air and waddled straight out of the gate, came round clutching her backside and created hell with my father. He went bananas, took the gun off me and smashed it to pieces out in the back yard. Frank also went mad and bashed me because I'd ruined his pride and joy. It was about the only time I really saw Father angry.

Even when I decided to see what was inside his false teeth he didn't create. I used to look at these dentures running across the front of his mouth and wonder how they were made. So one day I took them out into the yard and tapped away at them with a hammer, gently at first, then more viciously, until I completely smashed them up. I realized I'd made a balls-up, but he never said much about it, and didn't even bother to replace them. He spent the rest of his life without any teeth in the front of his mouth.

The Old Man was our main parental contact; we never really spent much time with Mother. As soon as school was over we'd be down the pier to see if he was in and while we waited we'd pester the men to teach us how to splice ropes and mend nets. The harbour was our playground; we mucked around in punts like other kids rode bicycles. We never thought much about it but, looking back, it was a perfect childhood.

Dad was the sort of chap who knew a little bit about everything, from the masses of useless knowledge he'd picked up on his trips around the world, and from the numerous books he read. He would never waffle or make facts up; he used to say to me, 'And when you don't know, you don't know!'

He was born in 1894, and could remember sitting on his father's shoulders to see Queen Victoria visit Plymouth. He fished on the last sailing drifters and joined the merchant navy on the first of the steam boats.

166

On one of his trips in the merchant navy Father jumped ship in Cape Town, pinched a push-bike belonging to a priest, and rode 1000 miles to Johannesburg to turn up on some distant relation's doorstep. This must have been quite an adventure in the 1920s.

The Old Man got on well with most people; he loved talking to anyone about all manner of subjects. It meant that we had an entrée into a whole area of society which was shut to many other fishermen's children in the village.

The local vicar was a great friend and they would spend hours discussing his thoughts and opinions. There was also a family called Garnier in Newlyn, whose son Peter later became editor of *Autocar* magazine. Mrs Garnier was a real gentlewoman who was something else when it came to painting and sketching. Mr Garnier was a wonderful man, really well bred, educated and with all the bearing that a time in the army had given him. He was quite fascinating to listen to, having been all over the world, including Canada prospecting for gold when he was a youngster, and he liked nothing better than to be there talking with my father. To be like the Old Man was, a fisherman-cum-merchant seaman holding forth with this posh man was quite something for a young boy to see. I was very proud of him. Because they got on so well, my mum went as the Garniers' cook, which was a strange situation really. The Old Man would be there upstairs chatting away with all the high society people they had to stay, while Mum would be running up and down the stairs with food.

I was given the job of breaking the eggs in their dovecote so they wouldn't be overrun by pigeons. I used to love going up to do this because I'd get five shillings every time, but also because the Garniers' house held another draw for me in the shape of a forbidden toy, an airgun. If Mr Garnier was around when I went over to break the eggs he'd sneak out with this airgun and say to me, 'Now, for sixpence, d'you think you can shoot one of these pigeons?' We'd set about scoring as many hits as possible. The noise of the rifle would bring Mrs Garnier out and she'd say very gently, 'Geoffrey, I do wish you wouldn't do that,' with a look which showed she'd tried stopping him many times before. Some days I'd walk away with six bob – a fortune forty years ago.

As I got older I got along with the Old Man better than I did with my brother. We used to go in the pub together and chat away about fishing and life. He was a great reader of the Bible, although he never made anything of it. No one in the house ever brought the subject up or discussed his beliefs, but the Bible was always there on the table. I don't think even Mother really knew what beliefs lay in his heart and head. I'm not sure whether he believed in the afterlife or not but on his deathbed he said something strange which has always haunted me.

I went to see him in his upstairs bedroom as I did every evening towards the end and he seemed much the same as he had been for ages, frail but no worse. He was sitting up in bed and he whispered to me to get his pipe. Then he gave me instructions to go out to the Fisherman's Arms to buy him an ounce of Condor Pigtail which is damn strong stuff, more like poison than tobacco, and a bottle of rum. I sneaked them upstairs past Mum and we sat yarning. I hated rum but we drank the bottle dry, until at about midnight when I said, 'Now look, Nicky, I reckon I'm bound away upalong now.'

He took a puff on the pipe and without any emphasis said, 'All right. I reckon I'll be switching over tonight,' and he took another puff.

'What have we to do with you?'

'Take me up and have me burnt. Then chuck me down the back of the old quay.'

It was May month 1970 and I was skipper of a small wooden trawler. When I walked down along the quay to board her the following morning Billy Stevenson stopped me.

'Now look, you can't go to sea today.'

He didn't have to tell me why. About half an hour after I'd left him, Father had switched over.

Frank and I went out with his ashes and scattered them over the sea from the back of the pier out to the Lowlee buoy off Mousehole, letting them trickle through our fingers as we steamed away. From then on when we didn't want other boats to know our plans, one would call the other on the radio and say, 'I'm just steaming out over the Old Man,' or, 'I'm just going in over Nicky,' and so one knew the other was on his way in or out of harbour.

The Old Man had never wanted me to go to sea. He was always urging me to learn a skill before I went off fishing – it really was a precarious business then. But I had the consolation that at least he'd lived to see me go from deckhand to mate to skipper, and I knew he'd been proud really.

I kept some of Dad's ashes in my wallet in the little place you keep stamps, but over the years they've gradually disappeared. I suppose there are bits of him all over the place now.

TOP The Old Man, 1935
ABOVE Dad with Peter Garnier and some local children

169

I missed him. To be quite truthful I idolized him. He had a view on every aspect of life and I always thought of him as a little bit of a philosopher. There was a contrast between his large figure and his gentle manner. His attitude to life was, 'It's always nice to be nice whenever possible.'

Whereas Mum was just someone who brought me food, washed my clothes and gave me frequent dressing-downs, I looked up to and was in awe of the Old Man. I'm sure part of it was the way he was completely in tune with anything to do with the water. When I was only about three years old, I was down in the harbour on the old quay and I must have made a run and gone over the side. I had enough sense to just catch the edge of the quay. Brother Frank says all they could see were my fingertips. As I fell, Dad threw himself across the quay flat on his chest, pinned my fingers with his hands, arms fully outstretched, and pulled me up. He was such a strong man.

He could always see danger coming and was prepared for it as if he had a sixth sense. I suppose I've picked up my attitude to those areas of life we don't really understand from him. I don't question religion or the supernatural; I like to just leave them be.

Religion was taken for granted as playing a part in most people's lives when I was a boy, even if it was nothing much deeper than going to church on Sundays. We had buildings for most varieties of Christianity in Newlyn then. Alongside the obvious Methodist, Wesleyan chapels we had the more exotic Apostolics, Plymouth Brethren and Christadelphians. As children we were forbidden to go up to the Apostolic church just above the old quay; they wouldn't allow anyone in who wasn't a member. So it automatically held the fascination of any forbidden fruit. On Sunday evenings we'd be down playing in the harbour and waiting until we'd seen the last of them entering the church; then we'd creep up to the big brown door and open it as quietly as possible. We were rewarded by the sound of wailing and would pause for a moment to drink in the eerie sensations. In front of us was a large heavy purple velvet curtain to keep the cold out which we'd pull aside just enough to peep around the corner and watch all the goings on. Strange sights and sounds were revealed: people we'd see about the town every day acting like possessed creatures from a different world. I used to love that slight tingle of fear brought on by the prospect of being caught, and the possibility of who knew what punishment, such was our imagination.

There used to be, still are to a certain extent, two sides of a fishing community and fishermen. Some are very religious, Godfearing people; others apparently live by no set of rules or morals, get drunk and generally bum around. There was an automatic involvement with the churches a hundred years ago because they were the only places in Newlyn which provided entertainment of a Sunday. Now there's television and music and discos instead. But I'm pretty sure that the religious influence is still there in most sailors, even if it's hidden deep down. I don't think there are many who've been out here in rough weather, slid down the side of a mountainous sea, braced against the impact and haven't said aloud 'God!' Many a time when I've pushed things a bit too hard and I know I've been lucky to get back into the harbour I've felt that He's given us a little extra help.

The sea puts us fishermen closer than most people to danger from the elements. A racing driver lives dangerously, but it's in contact with man-made things: cars and engines and racetracks. We live *in* the elements, and the source of our livelihood can also kill us. When you're coming home in a storm everyone goes very quiet. Many times I've wondered if I've left it too late to get back. Should I have had one less haul and headed home earlier? And although other skippers might laugh and rubbish this in public, don't be fooled. Privately I suspect most of them would share my feelings. Everyone out here has to have something to hang fast to.

There was a boat out of Newlyn called the *Trevessa*, a sixty-five footer, which was caught in a storm out in the Channel and lost all radio contact. The news spread around that she'd gone and they even went as far as to tell the wives that there was no hope. But she came through it. The boat had been swamped by a mountainous sea and lost all its aerials just after they'd been on the radio describing how bad the conditions were. When I saw Ian, the youngest of the crew, he admitted he had been petrified. He told me that he'd got down on his knees and prayed. Lots of the others round the port laughed and joked about Ian, 'That silly bugger down on his knees,' but as far as I'm concerned that little bit from him might have made the difference to bring them home.

There are too many happenings in the world which can't be explained. This week they claim to have solved the origins of the universe by proving the Big Bang theory, but I sit up here in the wheelhouse of a night and ask myself what was there before the Big Bang? Then I lie in my bunk and think, OK, now we know about the universe, but what's beyond it?

171

There's a lot of superstition tied up with fishing; an attempt to explain bad luck or to harness outside forces to create good luck. Those old superstitions have always fascinated me.

Mentioning pigs or rabbits is still considered to bring bad luck, and anything going wrong will be blamed on the use of the forbidden words. Seeing a nun or a vicar is a bad one as well. There was a skipper in Newlyn who took this so seriously that when two sisters in full habits came down the pier and looked down into his boat one day, he refused to go to sea.

Most of the men don't like their women coming down on the pier to wave them goodbye. The origins of that superstition are lost; some say it has to do with the case at the turn of the century up in Grimsby when a fishing boat was waved off by the crew's wives only to disappear. After a year had passed everyone was convinced she'd been lost somewhere off Iceland, and some of the wives even remarried. But the fishermen had not been lost, just trapped in the ice, and had survived by eating seals and fish. When the thaw came they stripped everything wooden from their cabins, even the wooden deck, and burnt it in the boilers so they could limp back towards Grimsby. They were found and towed in by another boat only to discover that most of the families had already got over their loss. Who knows whether that's why men today get twitchy about being waved off, but the superstition certainly continues.

Gold is supposed to bring good luck. Fishermen wear something gold like a ring or an earring so that if they are lost at sea anyone discovering the body can use the gold to pay for a burial. This has always struck me as a waste of time since it's fairly obvious that most bodies would simply be relieved of their gold and left to rot.

In my younger days I kept all my nail clippings in little silver boxes so that no one could get hold of them to use against me. I don't do it any more after Nell complained that she was fed up with them being around the house, so now I use an emery board to make sure there's nothing left to be tampered with.

When I was younger I was so fascinated by witchcraft that I grabbed every opportunity to get near anything to do with it. Just outside Newlyn there was a house owned by a chap who took a great interest in the life and writings of the self-titled Great Beast, Aleister Crowley. He was an infamous black magician who was into devil worship, tarot cards and all manner of witchcraft, and generally lived an exciting life of debauchery. Crowley stayed in

Newlyn for a while in the Thirties, so there were people around who'd spent time with him and one chap we knew became obsessed by him. It took over his life to the extent that he fitted out the basement of his imposing mid-nineteenth-century house with swords on the walls, a long polished refectory table, and high-backed intricately carved chairs, all looking as though they could well have been set up for a coven meeting. The bleats of Demeter, the goat who was tethered outside, use to float through the hallway adding to the eerie atmosphere. Above the mantelpiece he had a painting of himself in full black magic regalia as his alter ego, Count Darkwise.

Frankie and I were drawn to the house regularly when we were in our late teens. On one visit we made our way down the steps, along the dark corridor and through the door into the meeting room where 'Count Darkwise' was looking intensely at the large, shining sword which he held in his hand.

'I want you to stand in front of me while I hold this sword to your throat,' he ordered me, not taking his eyes off the gleaming, sharp weapon.

My fears were alleviated only a little when he explained that he wanted to look in the mirror to judge how effective the pose would be as a cover picture for a book he was writing. So without taking my eyes off the sword I had no real choice but to agree. Frankie didn't know whether to laugh, scream or run, but noticeably he didn't offer to take my place.

We were once in the huge kitchen at about one o'clock in the morning having a drink and a yarn when we were disturbed by an unexplained sound. Above the swishing of the large trees which lined the long entrance drive, and the bleats of Demeter who was chained up to one of the trees, we heard a crunching noise which sounded like something large moving along the gravel. Not surprisingly, few visitors ventured inside the gates to sample the house's unwelcoming atmosphere, so this was a sinister sound. We were convinced someone or something would appear around the corner and inflict some terrible damage on us. I grabbed one of the heavy swords which hung all over the place, and stood ready to ward off the intruder.

The lady of the house stopped me, quite gently.

'Oh I shouldn't worry about that noise. It's only Mother coming home in her carriage to see us.'

A while later I was talking to one of the neighbours who expressed no surprise at this story. She told me how she'd been into the house when the old lady was still alive and had been overwhelmed by a heavy smell of flowers, although none could be seen anywhere.

Three or four days later the mother died and the neighbour went back up to pay her respects. Exactly the same smell was present, except this time it came from masses of flowers covering the coffin.

Sitting up here in the wheelhouse on my own in the middle of the night with nothing but darkness surrounding me, I'm getting the creeps just thinking about that place. I'm sure a lot of the sinister memories I have of the place and people have fermented in the memory over the years, but it's not the only encounter with spirits I've had.

When I was with Jenny, and Demelza was a young baby, I couldn't wait to get off the boat and rush home to see them at Perran Downs where we lived in her old man's bungalow. Demelza was usually asleep by the time I got home and Jenny would go mad if I woke her up to see her. So my first move was always to sneak into the bedroom and nudge Demelza so she'd wake up. One night I'd managed to innocently disturb her and we were there at two o'clock sitting in the kitchen feeding her an ice lolly. Our two huge wolfhounds were wandering around when suddenly one stopped in his tracks. His tail thickened up like a brush, his back arched and he growled menacingly, something he never did. I thought he just wanted to go out so I went to open the hall door and at the end of the hall by Jenny's dad's door there was a shape moving. If the dog hadn't reacted in such a strange way I would have thought I was seeing things. I backed into the kitchen at great speed.

'There's something down there.'

'I shouldn't worry about that,' Jenny said without looking up. 'It's probably Mother come down to see Demelza.'

Considering her mother had been dead several years this matter-of-fact response got the wind up me. Even thinking about it now is making me twitchy. I think I'll just nip back to the galley, make myself a coffee and check that the others are all tucked up safely in their bunks.

 WE WERE JUST off Lundy when we had a call on the radio: we were to steam up the coast to Wales to pick up a boat which had broken down. It was only when we were under way that we heard it was Brother whose gear box pump had gone. His boat is Irish, the *Deirdre Marie*, working between here and Dunmore East.

When we arrived she was wallowing in a deep swell which must have made things pretty unpleasant. I have a strange dream about having to go in and save a ship in ferocious weather as she nears treacherous rocks, and is about to founder. It's just about the only challenge I can think of which still excites me. But it was not to be today, Frank's tow was very straightforward.

As we came within sight of Newlyn I thought I'd have some fun at his expense and called him up on the radio. 'In all the years we've been at sea, Bro', how many times have I had to tow you in?' I waited for his reply, which was slow in coming. 'I don't know, a couple I suppose.' I grinned at Jiggy who knew Frank'd not like being reminded that his younger brother had come to his rescue too often for his liking. 'And how many times have you towed me in?' I persisted. I knew that it had only been once. 'Well, Bro', quite a few times really.' I could imagine Frank getting agitated, knowing that everyone would be listening in on this conversation.

But blow me – it served me right for gloating – before I could press the point the rope snapped, and we nearly lost him on the rocks by Mousehole, which might have made my dream come true but would have been very embarrassing. We attached another rope and, face saved, steamed the last mile towards the gaps.

It's always a tense moment when you tow a boat into the harbour, especially if she's lost steerage, which is quite common. As you get close to Newlyn you see people lined up on the quayside watching and you know they'll be hoping you'll hit the wall so they've got a good story to tell in the pub. The only people willing you through the gaps are the owner and the insurance company.

The spectators were disappointed today, though. In fact, the worst part was dealing with Brother on the pier once we'd landed.

I started joking that we looked forward to receiving the £3000 we'd lost by stopping fishing to tow him in, but he wasn't in the mood for jokes because he was supposed to be in Ireland for a wedding that night. Instead he started moaning about the way that he always got lower prices on the Newlyn fish market than us because he was a foreign boat. I told him that was a load of rubbish; the simple reason was that the fish from the Irish side of the sea aren't as good as ours, but he wouldn't accept it. The fact is the soles he catches are black and buyers just aren't interested in them. After about an hour's discussion we agreed to differ and parted.

I seem to have spent a good deal of time towing them in this year. Four months back I had to fetch nephew Stephen's eighty-foot trawler, *Sempre Allegro*, from up off the north coast. It was a big blow for him and his brother Michael because they bought the boat four years ago and have been working all hours possible to make it pay. They've had a lot of bad luck with mechanical troubles and as far as I can tell were only just about paying off the interest on the loan when the whole lot blew up, forcing a couple of months in port while the engine was repaired. It's bad enough for those of us who work for the Stevensons when a boat breaks down. We don't get paid anything unless we catch fish, but at least we don't have any outgoings for the boat. Stephen and Michael still had to keep up payments on a huge £200,000 loan for the *Sempre* as well as all their family expenses, with no money coming in.

It makes me appreciate the fact that I work for the company. When we are catching fish, we have a system of payment, called sharing, which is vastly better than at other ports. When I was in Lowestoft after I got my ticket, only the skipper and the mate received a real share of the catch money, and that was after all the boat's expenses had been taken out. The skipper was on around ten per cent and the mate would be on about seven, while the crew would have a wage of about £30 a week plus, if they were lucky, one per cent of the profit – just about enough to pay for their tobacco.

In Newlyn the traditional method on the pilchard driving boats was that each member of the crew owned a few nets which they would take on board whichever boat they worked, while the owner supplied the rest. Then they'd share out the catch money in proportion to the amount they contributed, after the boat's running expenses had been taken off the top.

When old Willie Stevenson started trawling he decided to give the crews on his boats a straight share of the catch after some expenses were removed, although they didn't have to bring their own equipment aboard. So now the skipper gets seven per cent, the mate six, the crew five each, down to a new young deckhand who might get two and a half per cent, which is pretty good really.

Luckily for my nephews, the insurance company paid up and they've gone back to sea to continue the slog to pay off the loan.

 WHEN I CAME on board this morning I went aft to make myself a cup of tea and I thought I was seeing a ghost. Tony was sitting in the corner with his head in his hands, looking greyer than the front page of *The West Briton* newspaper. Mitch told me that they were in the Ship Inn over in Mousehole last night until the early hours and that Tony was pouring alcohol down his throat like there was no today. He was certainly paying for it this evening now that we're back at sea. The *William Sampson* does not have the most pleasant sea motion at the best of times; with the effects of alcohol added she can be a pig. Tony turned in as soon as we left the harbour and I didn't expect to see him when we first shot the nets but, all credit to him, he dragged himself out of his bunk and was on deck when we shot.

When the nets were in the water and we were towing along nicely at about four knots, I went aft to the galley and heard Jiggy having a go at Tony in the galley.

'You should be like me; don't drink!' preached Jiggy in a sanctimonious tone, his indignation spoilt by the fact that he winked at me as he said it. 'Why d'you do it, Tony boy?'

'It's nice when you're doing it,' Tony mumbled, not quite believing himself. 'It must be something to do with the relief of being back on shore. You have a pint and bit of a yarn with the lads. Then another pint . . . ,' he rubbed his head continuously as he spoke. 'And then you start to get nagged by the missus, and things get worse.'

'You know your trouble, Tony, you get too easily trapped in corners.'

'You're dead right, Jiggy. I got trapped in a corner last night.'

'How are you doing, old boy?' boomed Mitch as he stood outside the galley door removing his oilies. Tony winced at the impact of Mitch's voice.

'Right at this minute I'd rather be a million miles away. But you learn by your mistakes, Mitch.'

'You should be a genius by now then, boy,' Mitch's bellowing laugh couldn't have helped Tony's head much.

Fishermen seem to have the need to drink large quantities of alcohol as soon as they come ashore. I'm sure Tony's right, it's partly relief at being ashore, partly just unwinding. Often we'll have been up all night landing the fish and won't have eaten, so

Graham and Tony waiting for the net to come in

the effects of alcohol are exaggerated, which usually leads to another few pints being consumed by mistake. The pleasure of that first pint ashore is wonderful, and tends to shorten the memory of the negative effects.

We never drink alcohol on board this boat; it would just be too dangerous. One moment's lack of concentration could lead to untold damage to man and machine.

The same cannot be said of all boats. We were in the harbour one day preparing to go to sea when we heard one of our trawlers, the *Filadelfia*, call for the lifeboat to meet it in the bay to help tow in a Spanish trawler which had broken down. The lifeboat went out to be greeted by the Spanish crew who were all along the rail swaying, so drunk they could hardly stand up. They were that inebriated that when the lifeboat went alongside, one of the crew had his fingers over the rail and as the boats came together they were chopped off.

Most of the foreign boats have booze on board. They probably need it to survive the living conditions on some of them. I've been on Spanish boats where the men live in conditions you can't imagine – one where three of the crew's bunks were *in* the engine room! Bobby often said on board here that we live a life worse than convicts, because at least in prison you have some privacy and get let out for a walk, but I don't know how some of those crews survive. They endure sleeping quarters that a homeless person

living on the streets wouldn't give a second look to; and they eat food that wouldn't be allowed in the most primitive soup kitchen – one pot on the stove with all sorts of fish ends bubbling away in it, heads, guts the lot, and alongside it some of the most evil wine you can imagine. Mind you, after you've had a few glasses of the rough, evil-tasting wine, even the fish stew tastes good.

Of course it would be unfair to say they're all like that. The new generation of French and Belgian trawlers put our rust buckets to shame and some of the French fishermen have always taken their food seriously, carrying very fresh supplies indeed.

A few years back we were out at sea on a Saturday, which was very unusual in those days, when we came across a French crabber called the *Marie Claire*. We called across to the crew to ask if they wanted a few of our gurnards for bait. They put out their fenders, we moored alongside, and we went aboard her. The boys went below to have a few beers with the French crew, while I sat up in the wheelhouse with the old man. Before too long we'd shared a bottle of wine and moved on to the Ricard.

When we'd climbed on board I'd noticed two hutches on this crabber's afterdeck. One was empty, the other held a large rabbit, a Belgian hare really I suppose. It looked very sad, with one ear up, the other down, having been cramped up in this tiny world on a moving platform for several days by then. As the effects of the alcohol made me feel mellow I thought about this poor creature, which was not being kept as a pet for sure.

I was parlez-vousing with the skipper and asked him what he was going to do with the animal. 'Ah!' his eyes lit up, 'tomorrow!' and he pulled his finger across his throat, 'Mange, mange!' Suddenly the idea of this poor thing being topped was too much for me. I pointed to the rabbit and then at my chest, 'For me?'

The skipper thought for a moment and then made an eating sign, 'Very good!' licked his lips and nodded in agreement.

'Yes,' I smiled back. I didn't mind if he thought I was going to eat it. Taking pity on the poor Brit who obviously ate so poorly, he exchanged this rabbit for some of our fresh vegetables and beef.

It came aboard into the wheelhouse and started thumping the floor with its foot, presumably a warning sign that hares make, but it soon settled down. It obviously had its sea legs because it was soon running around happily. I kept it in a fish basket alongside me in the wheelhouse, and it lived like a king on our fresh vegetables. It was not an altogether popular move with the crew, bearing in mind that there's a taboo against even *mentioning* rabbits on a fishing boat, let alone having one running around the deck.

The next day we lost one of our hooks and had to arrange to borrow one from another boat. I knew the skipper, Ernie Hunter, to be superstitious so as we came alongside I put the rabbit on my shoulder, went out on the wheelhouse wing and waved at him. He waved back, then paused and rushed into his wheelhouse to get his binoculars to inspect us more closely. Then he went bananas.

As we manoeuvred closer I let the rabbit down on our deck where it hopped around quite happily. Ernie also hopped around not so happily, getting very hot and cross. 'Don't let that bloody thing on board here!' he shouted, never taking his eyes off it. As soon as he'd passed the hook across he ran into the wheelhouse, opened the throttle wide and stormed away at full steam.

This was many years ago, before we were aware of the dangers of rabies, and I'd grown fond of the poor thing, so I did something I shouldn't have done. At the end of the trip I brought it ashore and took it into the pub on a lead. At first it went through its thumping the floor routine, but then it settled down, so we sat it up on the bar and gave it a saucer of beer. I happened to be talking to some friends, Mike and Maureen, who said they liked the sound of this maritime hare so they adopted it. It lived quite happily for several years, to a ripe old age.

We've always been a lucky boat and caught lots of fish so it didn't really bother us to have him on board, but some fishermen take the whole rabbits business very seriously. None more so than the coxswain of the ill-fated Penlee lifeboat, Trevelyan, or Whackers as he was called. He was the skipper of a fishing boat in Newlyn and he took all the taboos very seriously. Frank and I used to go out and do a bit of rabbit hunting in the fields above Newlyn. One day we took a couple of the dead animals out to sea with us and steamed off until we found Whackers.

He saw us approach and must have wondered what we were up to. When we were alongside him we threw the two carcasses on to his deck, which nearly made him burst a blood vessel. He ran out of the wheelhouse, threw them overboard and started shouting, 'I'll bloody murder you!' shaking his fist at us all the time.

I'm glad we had more horsepower than he did. I'm sure he would have jumped across and thumped us if he'd been able to.

OVERLEAF Sunset on the *William Sampson*

 WHEN I WENT into the galley after we'd hauled this morning you could have cut the air with a knife. They were all in there looking glum. I knew what had happened: Graham had been up to his tricks again. I'd overheard him needling the others while they'd been gutting the fish on deck.

This was due to be our last day at sea and he loves nothing better than to wind the rest up by saying that I've decided to stay out for longer. He knew that Mitch wanted to get back in for a party the following night, but also that none of them would say anything to me, accepting that it would be tough if it was true. Not wishing to spoil Graham's evil fun I said nothing, but left it for a while.

After the next haul I went back again and laid into all of them about someone pinching my Milky Way bars. I had my suspicions that one might have found its way into Mitch's mouth, but he was in such a foul mood that he wouldn't even turn round as I quizzed them all. With an impish smile, Tony owned up to having scoffed one of them, but no one else dared admit weakness. It was a great scene to observe, particularly when out of the blue I asked if we should have a vote on whether or not to go in early. Graham could hardly contain himself as he watched. Jiggy was all for it, 'Let's go home and see Mummy!' Mitch pretended not to be too bothered, 'It's up to you, Rog,' he replied gruffly and carried on leaning out the window. But I could see he was as excited as a small boy who's unexpectedly been let off school early. I always laugh to myself at the change in mood as soon as all hands know it's time to go back in. Jiggy takes on a new lease of life and almost shakes off his fifty-seven years in one moment; even Tony looks pleased.

The weather was getting worse and since it was our ninth day out we could justify returning to port. We needed to carry out a fair amount of work on the gear which would take the whole night, so we might as well do it in the comfort of the harbour, before landing the fish in the morning. We quite often do this when we're at the end of the trip and the weather is bad. It means we get some respite from being thrown around for another twenty-four hours, but don't lose any fishing. The boss is happy and the boys get their full time ashore before the next trip.

By the time we moored up there was an end of term feel about the boat. Even though we faced nearly twenty-four hours without sleep working on deck and landing the fish, we had a good catch to send up to the market and we'd soon be downing that first pint.

I wasn't disappointed when I went up to the office to pick up the cheque from Elizabeth Stevenson: monkfish did well, as did the soles. You don't mind working hard when you make decent money for it.

In the Star Inn after I'd settled up with the boys I wandered across to see Brother Frank who was having a yarn with the landlord and another deep water trawler skipper. Both had spent some time in the navy and started reminiscing about their early days on board a training ship. They compared notes on how harsh the life was, and mentioned the doctor in particular, who performed everything from teeth extractions to appendix operations on board. Frank rushed up home and brought back a photograph of an officer standing in front of a ship and asked them if they recognized either of them. They looked at it. 'That's the bugger!' The ship was the *Arethusa* and the man was the doctor, our Uncle Jim.

Jim was Dad's brother-in-law who'd met my Aunt Sue when she was a nurse. I could remember the stories he used to tell of his days in the navy on this training ship. Our early days at sea were tough but these lads had it even rougher.

He must have been pretty well off when he left the navy, because he gave up the sea and they came back to Newlyn, to live in what everyone calls 'The Big House', overlooking the harbour.

It was a great place for kids. There was an adit, a water tunnel, which went from under the house, several hundred yards down the hill, carrying rain water into the harbour. The walled garden was huge, with a path leading through neat rows of fruit and vegetables to a big cherry tree at the bottom. The strawberries were red, juicy and enormous, the gooseberries were slightly pink on one side and big as golf balls. We loved to pick a few on our way through, never thinking too much about why they were so big and so rich. It's only now that I can connect them with Aunt Sue's daily ritual mulching. She would walk between the rows, carefully distributing the contents of a white enamel bucket which she held by its wire and wooden handle. Potato peelings, banana skins and other remnants of food – everything went in there, nothing was wasted. There were other more potent growth promoters in there as well,

OVERLEAF High and dry in Newlyn Harbour

which meant you could smell that bucket long before Aunt Sue appeared with it on her pilgrimage, not surprising considering the bucket also served as the outside privy receptacle.

We went to Aunty Sue for dinner every day from school. Our first task would be to go up the hill to fetch milk from Minnie Winnie's farm. The churn held about half a gallon and if I let my arm fall down straight, the bottom would scrape along the floor, so I always took ages coming back, stopping to change this huge weight from one arm to the other every few yards. Aunt Sue used the milk to make her own rich clotted cream, which we'd then have with the strawberries. The only thing we were given to drink was Guinness and tonic water – the Guinness from the old screw-top bottles with a brown paper seal.

She was a funny old thing. Although they were well off they became obsessively careful as they grew older. If we were ever given an apple and lost interest in it, wandering off like kids do, she'd put the remaining piece under a cheese dish. We'd have to finish that before we could have anything else, despite the fact that the garden was often so overflowing with fruit that it rotted on the trees.

Uncle's obsession was tending the open fire which was started with coal and changed to coke as soon as it was going. He would spend all evening hovering over it and covering up any sign of red glowing coals with minute pieces of coke, so as to keep the heat in, I suppose.

You always had to behave yourself there – no running around or being frivolous – although we were allowed to wander around the house which was full of unbelievable treasure. Aunt Sue was in the habit of buying masses of wonderful furniture at auctions which she'd have delivered, put away in a room and never give a second thought to. All these rooms were shut up, while my uncle and aunt ended up living in one corner of this great house. There was one room which went all the way from the front to the back of the house. In it was a Persian carpet which had never been walked on, and a chaise longue which had never been used. Another room held a grand piano, and a large bear rug with the animal's head lying on the floor, gaping open in a grotesque roar. There were fur stoles complete with legs and heads, and hat-boxes full of who knew what bits and pieces, all untouched from the moment they came through the door. It was a real Aladdin's cave, especially the room with all Uncle's medical tools lying around: pliers for pulling out teeth, operating instruments and other savage-looking equipment. The only thing we were allowed to actually play with was the piano, because Aunt Sue knew that while she could hear us making noises we weren't up to anything else.

They were hoarders. Come the end there were rooms full of newspapers, all piled up neatly, while they lived a cramped life in one room.

Aunt Sue used to make all the clothes she wore: great thick skirts down to her ankles, with old fashioned cardigans. She looked like something out of the last century. They had money, but they never went out. Uncle Jim used to just sit smoking Senior Service, with his spittoon alongside him. Looking back, it doesn't seem much of an end for people who'd led such interesting lives, although I think they were happy in their own way.

It wasn't that they were mean – she was always generous to us children. If we were there when the mobile shop came to her house she would go out and buy not just one bar of chocolate, but the whole box; not a single liquorice pipe, but three cartons. I think the shop owner used to put out extra boxes on display in the van knowing he'd make a good sale at The Big House. She'd buy us a new pair of shoes in town and say, 'Now you try those on.' We'd try them and they'd fit beautifully. Delighted with this, she'd say, 'Well you can have them soon,' and promptly put them away and forget about them. Of course, if she did find them a couple of years later they would have become too small.

She just did not like throwing anything out. Every so often she'd say she was having a sort-out, and one small box of rubbish would appear in the dustbin. The only time she did throw any great quantity of things on a bonfire, she threw out my uncle's medals, the one who'd been shot in the First World War. Luckily we managed to retrieve them.

She also owned a large three-storey house in Plymouth which was completely boarded up. In my teens I was taken up on the train carrying paint brushes and paraffin to treat all the furniture in the nine or ten rooms to stop it from getting woodworm. When we got there the grass had grown up to the height of the windows and we couldn't budge the front door. I had to force my way in through a window and soon discovered why the door was jammed. Junk mail was piled up to the level of the letter box.

It's only now that I come to think about it that I wonder why they were like they were. As kids we used to just accept it, in fact it was great to have an uncle and aunt who were more interesting than all my pals' relations.

Uncle's last few years were very sad. His mind deteriorated until he had to be taken everywhere by Aunt Sue. In his younger days he'd been immaculate and spotless; as he neared his end his beard grew out like some old tramp's and his nails became so long they were like great talons. I used to have to light a fag up for him because his beard was so bushy that he would have set fire to himself. Every week Aunty Sue had to dress him up to take him into Penzance to get his pension. The poor old boy should really have been left alone. Even then I used to like going there, right up until he died in his nineties.

Near Aunty Sue's end she went the same way. I remember visiting her with my dad and she'd look at me and say, 'Now who's this young man, Nicky?' and he'd say to her, 'Now, come on, you know who it is. That's young Roger.' It was very sad and convinced me that I do not want to end up like that if I have any say in the matter.

With them both dead everything was sold up. When they turned out the attic it was full of clothes which were in pristine condition. Beautiful high heeled shoes from the 1920s, dresses she'd made, none of them worn. She'd put about £300 in a hat box, but it had been there for so long that it was all old, out-of-date currency.

The Newlyn house, with all these fantastic contents and furniture, most of which had never been sat on, was sold for £3000; the house in Plymouth went for less. It was shocking.

———————————

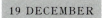

 TODAY MARKS THE eleventh anniversary of the most heartbreaking, unnecessary tragedy this part of the world has seen. I hope never to experience such a day again.

The weather was poor, at least a force nine, with the sea whipped up into a terrible state, and we were one of the last two ships of the fleet left out at sea. Then even we decided enough was enough and it was time to go home. As we steamed down the bay towards Newlyn at about six o'clock in the evening the big tug, which was always on standby off St Michael's Mount, was just heaving up her anchor. None of us thought too much about it, except that she must have been bound for a more sheltered anchorage at Falmouth up the coast. Mounts Bay is not a nice place to sit out a storm.

By the time I arrived home the strength of the wind had increased frighteningly. Nell and I lived on a farm just outside Newlyn and one of the interior kitchen doors was off being stripped. Nell had covered the opening with a heavy velvet curtain and the wind was causing such a strong draught through the house that it was lifting this curtain and making it billow and flap like a sail. We had to move a dresser up against the door frame to keep the drape in place. Unusually, a very heavy weather warning for the south-west flashed on the television and a little while after that we heard that the Penlee lifeboat had been called out. It was a real howler.

I can still hear Nellie saying, 'I wouldn't like to be out in that tonight!'

Without thinking too much about it, I said, 'Oh, they're all OK. They know what they're doing.' Looking back, Nellie's response was a strange omen.

'Well who goes out to the lifeboat if *they* get in trouble?'

It was such an inconceivable idea that I had to stop and consider it. I could only think that they'd have to call out another lifeboat, but it seemed academic because it would never happen. I knew the crew, all good fishermen who had more experience of the sea than most, particularly of the waters around our part of the coast.

We never gave it more of a thought. The next morning at about half past seven I was in bed when Nellie came running up the stairs and into the bedroom. She was white.

'Roger, Roger, the lifeboat's gone. Our lifeboat!'

The unthinkable had happened. The Penlee lifeboat *Solomon Brown* had foundered on the rocks with all eight hands lost. I rushed downstairs to switch on all the radios and the television. I knew all these men; I'd been to sea with some of them, and I could imagine it all happening to them out there only too well.

There weren't many details except that a coaster, the *Union Star*, had been having engine trouble, but had struggled for some time before requesting assistance from the lifeboat.

It had all been too late. The ship was so close to shore that the lifeboat didn't stand a chance. She was smashed against the rocks and broke up. We didn't know much more than that.

At ten o'clock that morning, when there didn't seem to be any fresh news coming over the radio, I went over to Newlyn and walked down the quay with brother Frank and nephew Stephen. Everything was quiet, no one talked. People were thinking about what had gone on out there, and we knew too much not to have an all too clear impression of the scene.

As we got to the end of the pier we saw Leslie Nicholls, a fisherman from Mousehole who was great pals with the coxswain of the lifeboat, Trevelyan. He was standing by the mouth of the harbour, his shoulders drooping in utter dejection. As we watched we saw that his eyes were following a small netter which was towing in the stern of the lifeboat. Without saying anything to each other we knew that we'd gone far enough. We turned around and went up towards the Dolphin pub.

On our way up the quay we met Billy Stevenson. 'I knew this had happened last night.'

I said, 'Well how the hell did you know that?'

Because of the bad weather he'd been down on the quay checking the mooring ropes of all his trawlers. Young Brocky, the son of one of the crew and a lifeboatman himself, had come down the pier. When the shout had gone up to launch the lifeboat, young Brocky wanted to get aboard with his dad, but Trevelyan said quite firmly, 'No, you aren't coming.' He didn't want two from the same family out on such a bad night. Later in the evening, listening on shore to the radio chat between lifeboat and coastguards, young Brocky had heard that the lifeboat had picked up some people and he'd come over to Newlyn to meet them.

On the pier he met Billy. 'Is the lifeboat here?'

When Billy said that it wasn't, young Brocky simply said, 'Well if she int here now she int going to be coming then.' He knew she'd gone.

Up in the Dolphin the atmosphere was eerie. In muted, sad, unbelieving tones people talked about what they thought had happened. Of course everyone had their views as to what and why and who was to blame. We had a few beers and I said that I was going over to Mousehole to see my friends. Just outside Newlyn a policeman I didn't recognize stopped my car and insisted that I could go no further. I was outraged: all my friends were there and I was being told I couldn't go to them. I think he could tell very quickly that he would have been foolish to stand in my way.

In Mousehole I went up to see Jimmy Madron, whose son Steven and two cousins had been lost. He opened the door, looked at me for a moment then just said, 'Come in here,' and took me through into the kitchen. As we went through the door he pointed, 'Look at that.' There above the Aga was Steven's old Breton peaked cap with the lifeboat badge sewn on its peak. He'd been walking on the beach that morning, just twelve hours after the lifeboat had gone down, when he'd seen the cap on the rocks.

Jimmy and I didn't say much that morning, but just sat and looked out at the sea where conditions were still bad. One of the worst sights, which still haunts me, was the flock of scavenging seagulls whirling around above the rocks where the wreckage of the ships was being constantly thrashed against the cliffs.

Steven's body was never found. On the opposite wall from his cap I looked up at the old sampler which had always hung there. Four white angels surround a poem:

> I cannot bend beside his grave
> for he sleeps in a secret sea,
> and not one gentle whispering wave
> will tell the place to me.
> But though unseen through human eyes,
> and humans know it not,
> his father knoweth where he lies,
> and the angels guard the spot.

It could have been written for Steven. In fact it had been made three generations earlier by the widow of John Thomas Madron, Jimmy's great uncle, who was lost at sea from a fishing boat called the *Aurora* in 1887 when they were up off Aberdeen on the herrings.

The poem has been tragically appropriate on several other unhappy occasions for the Madron family since then. At the turn of the century five more of the family were lost coming home from

the North Sea. All they found was the mizzen mast. Then his Grandpa's five nephews were lost off St Ives before Grandpa himself was lost off Plymouth.

When Jimmy was at sea in the Fifties there was another tragedy. Jimmy and his two brothers, Joe and Edwin, had been out pilchard driving off Plymouth with their father, Edwin senior. Joe fell over the side and brother Edwin went in after him, but he couldn't swim and got into trouble, so Jimmy jumped in as well. The two crew members left on the boat had to hold the wheelhouse door shut to stop their father coming out of the wheelhouse, else he would have gone in after them as well. Joe and Jimmy survived, but Edwin drowned. It could easily have been all four of them.

Although we'd been out at sea until just before the lifeboat was launched that night in 1981, we hadn't heard anything about a boat in distress. I couldn't understand why we hadn't picked up a Mayday call on the VHF emergency frequency, channel sixteen, which we always monitor.

Then, as more information emerged, the reason for this became clearer. The 1400 ton *Union Star* had been on its maiden voyage from Denmark to Dublin when the engine stopped because of water in the fuel. The skipper didn't send a Mayday, but tried to restart the engines while he parlez-voused with the owners about whether or not to take a tow from the tug. Although the tug stood by them, by the time they'd agreed to request a tow it was too late. The hurricane force winds were making the sea break over the coaster from stem to stern and the tug couldn't get a line on board her, so they launched the Penlee lifeboat.

I don't care what anyone says, but that delay did nothing to help those lifeboat men. If the boys had been able to give assistance earlier when the problem had just occurred, they would probably have had plenty of sea-room to manoeuvre in, and might have been able to save the crew of the *Union Star*. But hindsight is an unfair judge. The coaster's crew must have been exhausted from the beating they'd taken.

Instead, the *Union Star* was forced into a V-shaped gulley by the huge waves which were being funnelled in. The conditions were compounded by a massive backwash coming off the cliffs which was stirring up the sea. It must have been hell.

Jimmy Madron with his son's cap

I could imagine the lifeboat going in there only too well; pitch dark, with only the dull illumination in the cockpit and her red and green steaming lights. The lifeboat managed to take four of the coaster's people on board before she was washed right up on to the *Union Star*'s deck, then washed off again a couple of times. There was that much sea around they didn't really stand a chance.

We discovered from radio conversations that they'd managed to get the captain's wife and one daughter off and were going back in for the fourteen-year-old sister. I could imagine them all out there, Trevelyan asking the boys if they were happy to go back in for the younger girl, and the boys saying, 'That young maid's there. Let's have another run for her.' The tug captain saw the lifeboat rise high on the crest of a wave, silhouetted by the *Union Star*'s deck lights. The lifeboat then disappeared from his view, as though in the trough of a wave. Within seconds the *Union Star*'s lights were lost from his sight as the ship capsized towards the shore.

Nothing more was seen or heard of the lifeboat. All hands were gone.

The stern post of the lifeboat was found several miles away, off St Michael's Mount, which showed how bad the waves and tide must have been. The post had been pounded against the rocks with such ferocious force it was gouged and worn as badly as wood that's been knocked around for years, not hours.

The impact of the tragedy on people in the town was amazing. By midday a collection was started and you've never seen anything like it; there were buckets bulging with notes in all the pubs around. Not all lifeboat crews are as well respected, but then not all lifeboat crews know the sea so intimately as this one did.

I'd sailed with all these men, especially Steven Madron and Trevelyan. It was wrong that men so full of life had been lost so pointlessly. Trevelyan's sense of fun was well known. His favourite trick was to go down the quay and pick up a rat, put it in his pocket and go into the Bath Inn in Penzance, where all the fishermen used to go. They'd sit there having a few pints, then he'd pull this live rat out of his pocket, drop it on the floor and all the old dears would shriek as the rodent ran around the pub. He got me one night when we'd come in from sea and I was all in. As I dozed in the corner of the bar he got a straw and blew a wad of snuff up my nostril. I thought someone had cleaved the top of my head off, it was such a shock. But I got my own back on him.

He was quite a meticulous man who loved doing things like

196

putting ships in bottles, and making intricate rope knots. He couldn't stand anything out of place on his boat, especially anything that rattled. He'd jammed bits of cardboard and rope or wood wedges everywhere to stop annoying vibrations. One of the worst offenders was our old coal stove in the sleeping quarters. Every bit of it rattled, especially the doors, and he never slept until he'd finally got rid of every last squeak.

One night we waited for him to turn in, watched him climb into his bunk and pull his curtain across. We kept still for a few minutes then got out and removed the little wedges around the doors so that they started rattling again. Then we shot back into our bunks and watched. Next thing, Trevelyan's curtain would fly back, out would come the white seaboot socks, then his legs and the rest of his six foot six. He'd hit the stove, then find a bit of something to stop the noise, talking and swearing at it all the time. 'You won't rattle no more,' he'd mutter and give it a last thump before climbing back into his bunk.

We did this three nights running and the third time he got so mad that he put his foot right through the stove and kicked it clean off its stand, leaving nothing but the chimney, which hung there with all the soot dripping down.

One night after I'd become a skipper, we were tied up to the pier with another boat, the *Anthony Stevenson*, moored alongside us. Trevelyan came home in the *Excellent* and tied up outside the *Anthony*, three of us in a row. Bobby Sowdon was skipper of the *Anthony*, and he watched Trevelyan down on the deck working on the nets under the deck lights. Bobby went into his wheelhouse and shone the spotlight into Trevelyan's eyes, and flicked it on and off a few times. He kept doing this every few minutes. You could see Trevelyan getting madder and madder. I said to the boys, 'You watch, there's going to be hell on here in a minute.' Sure enough, it happened again and that was it. Trevelyan went up forward, got out a heavy lump hammer, walked across the deck of his boat, jumped on the *Anthony*, walked aft, climbed up the ladder, came across the top of the wheelhouse and smashed the spotlight to pieces, mumbling to himself all the time. Several hundred pounds' worth of equipment gone. He offered to pay for it but nothing more was said.

Trevelyan lived with his mother all his life, right into his fifties. He'd looked after her since his father died, and she'd looked after him just as she had done when he was ten. She never got over Trevelyan's death.

After the tragedy a huge amount of money was raised for the families but even that caused trouble when there was an announcement that it would all be taxed before the families got any of it. Everyone was dumbstruck and Maggie Thatcher had to step in to alter the score on that one.

It's strange how these events bring out the best and the worst in people. The gutter press were soon sniffing around looking for dirt to rake up on the men or their families.

I was in The Coastguard Hotel at Mousehole on the evening the Duke and Duchess of Kent came to visit the families. A reporter came up to me and asked if there was any truth that the crew were drunk when they went to sea. I looked at him, said nothing, then pushed him away and turned my back on him. But he kept on and on at me, even started tugging at my shirt.

I thought to myself, 'You do that once more . . .', but said nothing.

'Well, were they?' he persisted.

He'd tried once too often. I became so annoyed that I banged him one, and kept on at him, pushing him into the corner until two or three of the others had to pull me off. I could quite easily have damaged him very badly if they hadn't held me back. I said to him, 'Don't you come over to Newlyn tomorrow because there'll be hundreds of men there then. What I've done to you now will be nothing; they'll tear you apart.' He disappeared very swiftly.

After the disaster some people jumped on the bandwagon, revelling in others' misfortune. They wanted to get in on the act and, awful as it might sound, I'm sure a few almost wished something similar had happened to someone in their families. There were people who have never been prominent in any area of their lives and all of a sudden they could see a way of coming to people's attention by getting involved with the aftermath of the tragedy. Eleven years on that sticks in the throat.

When I was with Jimmy Madron the other day he offered me a rum, which I refused saying that the last time I'd had rum was the night before my Old Man died. Jimmy said, 'Well maybe he'd like one. He's just down there, isn't he?' pointing to the sea right in front of his house where we'd scattered Dad's ashes. I asked him, 'Where are you going to when you switch over?' He said, 'I'm not going up to the churchyard to be eaten by worms. I'm going up the shore with the boy.' Which I thought was just right.

 AFTER STEAMING FOR six hours, we've just arrived off the Welsh coast and shot the nets. The hundred fathoms, about six hundred feet, of warps trailing behind us are now towing the trawls along the seabed. I've been talking to a few of the skippers on the radio, trying to build up a picture of who's catching what where, but I'm less inclined to take much notice of what they say than I used to be. If anyone's found good fishing today they'll probably keep it to themselves. They'll say that there's not much about, but when you see their catch laid out on the market the next day, they've miraculously caught a boatload in their last couple of hauls.

Some skippers have always been like that. In my teens, when I was still working on the deck, I was fishing up off the Seven Stones with a skipper called George Lacey, and we were getting a good quantity of fish. Another boat appeared and started sailing towards us to come alongside and have a chat. As soon as George realized that they were closing on us he ordered us to throw the huge mounds of freshly caught fish lying on deck down into the fish room so that the other skipper wouldn't see how well we were doing. Then he shouted across, 'Nothing much around here, my handsome!' The other skipper looked down at our deck, which was empty apart from a few small fish, and steamed off to look for better grounds, leaving us a clear field. When he was out of sight we had to laboriously pull all the ungutted fish back up from the hold and gut them. We went through this many times with George.

This job is all about hunting, really. After thirty odd years you know the patterns of the fish movements through the seasons. One April you might find a bit of fish in a certain area, so come twelve months' time you try it again. We know that the big Dover soles move down the Bristol channel during the first quarter of the year, steadily down past Lundy along a fifty mile track. By the end of April we're catching huge female Dover soles full of roe, and then they disappear. That's the one mystery. Do they have a secret breeding ground or do they spawn and then disappear to die?

It's exciting when you find fish on a piece of ground that no one else has discovered. Nowadays with the French, Spaniards and Belgians listening on the radio you have to keep it to yourself. In fact I usually switch the radio off, say nothing and leave it at that.

There's more greed attached to the business today; it's very much dog eat dog out here. The camaraderie between skippers has all but disappeared. I suppose it's inevitable with more and more boats chasing smaller quantities of fish. What is there, is being caught more efficiently which means that one boat can catch what a whole fleet would have survived on in the past.

Sometimes when we're out in a force seven or eight, I lie in my bunk knowing we've got nine days of it ahead with little chance of catching half the fish we would normally, and wonder what it's all about. I've had a few small wins on the pools over the years and I'm sure if I had a half decent win I'd be off like a shot.

The job's become so boring today. In the old way of fishing there was a bit of an art. Now all the electronic navigation systems make it easier to steer the boat than it is to drive a car. We know to within a few hundred feet where we are all the time, and even have electronic charts on which I can draw a track so the watchkeeper simply has to steer along the dotted line like a big computer game. Then we pull a couple of levers and sit back for three or four more hours while the gear slams along the seabed. When we were side winding we'd have to launch all the gear by hand then after we'd finished gutting and sorting the catch we'd carry straight on to repair the next set of gear. The gear got smashed up a lot more because it was always getting caught and the nets constantly came up in rags, so sometimes you'd be on deck for three solid days, casting, hauling, gutting, casting, mending. It was a lot harder work but the time went far more quickly because you were always doing something. When you did manage to get down below you were so tired that you just fell asleep, flat out until the next haul. Now I sometimes get into my bunk and get up again after an hour because I just don't need the sleep.

I think back to when I was ten or eleven and I used to love to go down to the fishermen's rest on Newlyn's old quay just below where we lived. I was quite happy just sitting in the corner of this old hut, soaking up all the old men said about the finer points of navigation or a new type of net. It was so exciting and I couldn't imagine wanting to be involved in any other world. The rest was a great place where they'd spend all day, just nipping home for lunch. The windows were never opened even when the temperature was up in the eighties, so as they sat around playing draughts or dominoes and smoking their roll-ups or pipes, the place would develop a wonderful comforting smog. When the weather was fine they'd all come out and walk up and down the harbour wall in twos and threes, twenty or thirty feet apart, yarning to each other about the boats or the fishing. I can see them now in suits which were probably thirty years old when they bought them and would have stood up on their own. They had no creases, shiny elbows and knees, and were worn with a fisherman's sweater underneath and a trilby hat or peaked cap. I'd follow them as they walked and I was always amazed when every now and again they'd all stop at the same time, spread as they were along the length of the railings, and turn to lean and look out over the harbour. It was just like watching a flock of birds change direction at some secret signal.

There were two distinctive groups of people in Newlyn: Newlyn Towners, around where we lived and where the old boys hung out in the rest; and Street-a-Noweners at the other end of the harbour, all of five yards away. It was only five or six years ago that the Street-a-Noweners stopped meeting in the small shed in front of the harbour offices. Early in the morning the fish buyers would stand in a circle in this shed, looking at sample baskets of fish which were brought up from the boats to save them having to walk down the quay. Then each catch of several thousand tons of mackerel would go straight from the boat into the buyer's lorry.

Once the buyers had finished, the old men took over the shed. It kept them together after they'd finished going to sea, and gave them a contact with the fishermen. The shed's gone, and although the fishermen's rest is still there down on the old quay there aren't any old fishermen to go there now. The one or two that are around sometimes spend an hour in the new mission building in the town, but it's a very different building, and a very different industry with very different problems from the ones the old boys faced.

Things beyond our control affect fishing. When I hear that another mine is to close down I can't help wondering how long before we feel the knock-on effect. If you look at the chain we use on our trawls, it's worn flat on one side where it's already been used in mines to riddle out coal. As the mines close down we're going to have to buy brand new chain which will cost a fortune. Added to this, all the electronics we carry mean more expense on the boats, and I fear that youngsters in particular will stay out in poor weather just to get those few extra baskets of fish to cover their expenses. While they're out, we have to stay with them, or lose out ourselves. These big beam trawlers will take bad weather without any problems, but the strain on the men is terrible. It's all so futile because we're not making much money anyway. I feel really sorry

---

OVERLEAF Looking across the old quay at Newlyn

for the men with the smaller boats, trying to work in gales in boats which are just too small to take it. They don't have much choice either if they want to fish because the licences for larger boats are few and far between and when they do come up for sale the cost is astronomical. So they have to stay in smaller boats and work away until they can save enough to jump up to the next size.

It all seems to revolve around money now. I wish I could regain some of the excitement I used to feel when I was first at sea. I would dash up on the whaleback at the bow of the ship to watch the warps being pulled in through the water and as the net emerged my mind would work overtime imagining what sorts of fish were in it. As it neared the surface the catch would bubble in the sea, and it was really exciting. That's not to say that all hands don't watch the cod end swing inboard, but now it's more a case of calculating how much that particular haul is going to be worth or looking to see if the net's damaged. I don't know what proportion of fishermen are brilliant mathematicians, but when it comes to making a mental calculation – how many sole at this price and how many monkfish at another – most of us are pretty agile. Within a few moments of the net being emptied the tally is completed, and we know that yet again we haven't made our fortune.

This job is only satisfying now when you're making big prices at auction; something like £15,000 a trip. But of course when prices are low, so are you. Take the period of the Gulf War for example, prices went through the floor. A few weeks before it all started we went in with thirty-nine boxes of fish and made £5000. During the war we went in with three hundred boxes and it sold for just £13,000. Prices are always dependent on outside factors, but for some reason the Gulf War had a devastating effect. A French restaurateur over here on holiday told me that there were no Americans in his restaurant, and generally less tourists. That, multiplied across Europe, depressed fish prices in Newlyn.

I'm hoping the area we're working this evening will prove to be good ground. There are one or two ships around on the radar. Enough to make me feel there must be something here, but not too many to have been across this ground and laid it barren. Most of them are Belgian beamers judging by the radio conversations. Time to turn in and leave Mitch to take the next watches. Most skippers like to be in their bunks soon after midnight and stay there until about eight o'clock the following morning. Privilege of rank, I suppose, making up for all the years spent working on deck around the clock. I shall dream of that big pools win.

THE BOWLER-HATTED, BEARDED FIGURE moved through the packed Ship Inn carrying the Starry Gazey Pie with its mackerel heads and tails poking out through the pastry. If any visitors were in any doubt as to what was going on, the song sung as the pie was handed around explained the ritual of Tom Bowcock's Eve in Mousehole – as strong a tradition as the Furry Dance in Helston or the Obby Oss in Padstow. Along with the lights in Newlyn and Mousehole this is the start of Christmas festivities down here. With Graham, Tony and what seemed like most of the rest of the Newlyn fleet it turned into quite a session.

The end of the year hasn't brought us good fortune on the *William Sampson*. Another engine breakdown saw us back in port early, with the prospect of several weeks ashore while a part is sent over from Holland. Mitch has damaged his back and is off to a hospital in London trying to get it fixed. It may not make any great difference to any of us since we face a new set of MAFF regulations in the New Year which look likely to keep us tied up in harbour for a week every month as part of the conservation bill. No one seems to know for sure what new rules will appear, so we wait to see what the final restrictions will be. I can't help feeling that I may end next year working in the small tosher, out lining for a few mackerel.

Even sadder from my point of view, Bobby Button has finally decided to hang up his oilskins; the doctors say they can do nothing to improve his arthritis-induced dizzy spells, so he's better off ashore. I'll miss him, and I don't know who Jiggy will argue with now, but I must say the old boy looks better than he ever has done. Inez was telling me that from the moment he wakes up he is playing practical jokes on her. Retirement has obviously given him a new lease of life.

I still don't know what will happen about my little discussions with Her Majesty's tax inspectors – but since she's now decided to pay tax herself, I suppose I might have to cough up as well!

Fishermen end the year with the dubious honour of having the most dangerous job in the country, 700 per cent worse than even the few miners who are left. I can believe it. We were involved ourselves in a search for what will hopefully be the last tragedy of the year, up off Padstow just last week, when yet another ship was lost with all hands. During the year nearly thirty fishing boats

went down, over twenty fishermen lost their lives, and nearly 300 non-fatal accidents happened on fishing boats: the numbers say it all.

Despite this I know that within a few days of being ashore I'll be missing the sea and desperate to get back out through the harbour gaps. I have no doubt that Nellie will be waiting for me to go back as well – I know I'm not the best of company when I've been ashore for too long, and even she will be happy for me to rush back to my other family and into the arms of the other woman in my life, the sea.

Then it won't be long before Jiggy starts moaning about something or other again: 'It's a lash-up Roger, a lash-up!' And don't I just love it!